ESCAPE FROM HOLY HILL
A Nun's Tale

JOANNE BRASIL

A BROWN FEDORA BOOK

Praise for *Escape from Billy's Bar-B-Que:*

"…how much pleasure *Escape from Billy's Bar-B-Que* has brought me, and just in my hour of need!" Spalding Gray

"To those who have wanted to dismantle racial pigeonholes and leap over social barriers in a single bound, this book will offer special insight and encouragement." Alice Walker

"… a valuable reminder that hearts and times do change, and for the better." Gloria Steinem

"This fragile novel packs a surprising wallop you'll feel for a long time afterward." *San Francisco Chronicle*

"Brasil has written a brilliant story…" *Publishers Weekly*

"… a little gem, a real jewel As Mayor of Cambridge, I once awarded Ms. Brasil a Key to the City of Cambridge for her contribution to our city and its literature. And she has a key to our hearts." Ken Reeves, Mayor/City Councilor, Cambridge, MA 1990-2007

"Brasil's story is both hopeful and convincing, and given the size of the social walls Cecyl runs into this is no small accomplishment… perceptive and well-written." *The Daily Californian*

"… for Tidewater residents, reading about Phoebus with its old veterans from the VA Hospital stopping in at Billy's 'for free empty jars to take to the bootleg house' is good fun." *Hampton Roads Daily Press*

"Hugely entertaining." *Mother Jones*

Other books by JoAnne Brasil

Escape from Billy's Bar-B-Q

Hildegard's Wander Theater

Fish Tacos to Go

BFB

A BROWN FEDORA BOOK

Brown Fedora Books is a writers' consortium,
publishing books that are
"Rebar Tough and Built to Last."

SALEM, Massachusetts/Portland, Oregon/Genoa, Italy

ISBN: 9781091662537

Chapter 1
"1945"

"You have your whole life ahead of you," Mrs. Reilly shrieked. "A convent? Don't you want to get married and have babies like other girls?" No, Edna wanted to marry Christ. She would join a cloistered order of Catholic nuns who were also married to Christ, and live behind brick walls largely in silence. "Is this the best you can do?" Mrs. Reilly asked one last time, one last futile time before it was too late but it was already too late. Edna was 18, of legal age. She'd already made her plans. God had called her. It was God's will. "Please, Edna," she begged, "this makes no sense. We're not even Catholic!" But Edna wanted to be Catholic. She wanted to be part of something bigger than herself.

Mrs. Reilly lit a cigarette, took a few puffs, and fixed herself a Tom Collins Cocktail. She called it a Tom Collins: fizzy water, gin, an ice cube and a dash of bitters. She didn't know what bitters were but that bottle of bitters had been in her refrigerator since her husband died. So, what the hell? Plop, plop. Edna hated to see her mother smoke cigarettes and drink cocktails. Cocktails made her mother unapproachable and the whole house smelled like an ashtray. And knowing how judgmental her daughter could be, Mrs. Reilly drank and smoked in secret, pouring her cocktails into coffee cups and smoking in the bathroom of her Master Suite with the window opened just a crack.

This was how Mrs. Reilly passed her evenings and her afternoons. After Edna left, she started her mornings listening to Arthur Godfrey on the radio, and drinking her coffee with a little *splash*. Sometimes Arthur Godfrey would play the ukulele and sing. Sometimes he had guest singers like Miss Patti Page the Singing Rage, or Rosemary Clooney. Mrs. Reilly loved singing along with the radio:
> *Shine on, shine on harvest moon, up in the sky.*
> *I ain't had no lovin' since January, February, June or July.*

Mrs. Reilly sang and along. Why not? Why the hell not? Everyone in her family was gone. Her son and husband both died during the War. And now Edna was one of a dozen young women preparing to marry Christ at the Little Sisters of the Perpetual Rosary of Berkeley convent, up in the Berkeley Hills. The convent wasn't that far from El Cerrito but Mrs. Reilly had to take two buses to get there. She didn't have a car. But it was 1945. Most people didn't. In bad weather she took taxis. She thought of buying a car just to see Enda. But it didn't seem worth it since she was only allowed to see her daughter on a few sacred holidays, and then only from the *visitors' gallery*. "She might as well be on the goddamn moon!" Mrs. Reilly muttered to herself and lit another cigarette.

It was November and getting chilly out. At least Mrs. Reilly wouldn't have to open the window when she smoked a cigarette, now that Edna was gone. And when the Angostura Bitters on the refrigerator door were all gone, she bought a bottle of maraschino cherries--much better. Plop, plop. At least there was a liquor store just a short walk away and the walk always did her good. At least the War was over.

1945, Continued

1945 seemed to go on forever, though. By VE Day (Victory in Europe) half of Europe was in ruins. Six million dead here, 20 million dead there. In Asia after VJ Day (Victory over Japan) it was the same. A few million here, a few million there. It added up. Edna's brother and father were two of them. Her older brother Edwin was killed in the Atlantic when his ship was torpedoed by a German U-boat. He was 18. "If I had been born a boy like Edwin, I could be dead, too," she said to herself. That's war. Some people have to die; some people have to live, and pick up the pieces and bury them. But there were no pieces of Edmund left to pick up. He was buried at sea. The day after Edwin's memorial service, Edna's father died of a heart attack in the living room. He was 49.

After the shock wore off Mrs. Reilly mixed herself a Tom Collins and poured it into a frosty glass with two Maraschino cherries--

plop, plop--and started listening to Arthur Godfrey on the radio, singing along with Rosemary Clooney:

Shrimp boats are a comin' the sails are in sight,
Shrimp boats are a comin' there's dancin' tonight...

And to compensate for being alive when her brother and father were not, Edna decided to devote her life to God and enter a convent. She joined the Order of the Little Sisters of the Perpetual Rosary of Berkeley up in the Berkeley Hills, up at the end of the bus line on Grizzly Peak. Only one bus went there per hour. Not many people wanted to go to Grizzly Peak. It was too windy. But Edna didn't care about the wind or weather conditions outside.

Inside her new home in the convent Edna felt safe, safe from her mother and the clouds of sad cigarette smoke, and from the world and its wars and death. Edna didn't enter the convent to be safe, though. She entered the convent to be closer to God but inside this convent, she did find a new kind of security. She found a new home with a *new mother*, Mother Superior. She had no father or brother; but she had a new mother, many sisters, and a choir!

One day Edna started singing--like her mother used to do, but with the choir. The choir neatly absorbed Edna's squeaky and often off-key soprano voice. Edna was happy to rejoice with her fellow Sisters. And she loved the hymns:

Sons of God, hear his Holy Word.
Gather round the table of the Lord,
Eat His body, drink His blood,
And we'll sing a song of love!
Hallelu, hallelu, hallelu, hallelujah!

Chapter 2
"1952"

Mrs. Reilly had had one boy and one girl just a few years apart, just right. Now Edmund was in heaven and Edna was in the Little Sisters of the Perpetual Rosary convent. She had to let Edwin go, but she refused to give up on Edna. All through her pregnancy with Edna Mrs. Reilly had read poetry to her little fetus, especially poetry from her then favorite poet Edna St. Vincent Millay; and named her baby girl *Edna* in her honor. Maybe Baby Edna might become a poet one day, too. And then there was *Edna Ferber*, the novelist. Maybe Edna could become a novelist one day!

"You have a poetic spirit and you were always such a good reader, and you were was such a cute baby," Mrs. Reilly recalled. She was writing a letter to her daughter. "You were round-faced and red-headed. You smiled easily and almost never cried, not much at all," Mrs. Reilly reminisced while she wrote, adding a few suggestions for Edna's future. "U.C. Berkeley is close to your convent. You could still get in! You were smart; it's not too late. Why not go over and just take a look? Your convent is right on the bus line. Think it over."

Eleanora Reilly wrote to her daughter every day; but Edna never wrote back. Why not? Didn't she get those letters? Mrs. Reilly kept writing anyway. Whenever she came up with a new idea, she sent it off. "You always enjoyed typing. You were a great typist in high school. And shorthand, you'd be good at that. You could be a court stenographer, marry a nice guy and start a family. Or be a nurse. Then you'd have something to fall back on if your husband got sick or something, God forbid."

She wished she could at least TALK to Edna, maybe go out for lunch once in a while; but this was impossible. Her daughter was in a cloistered convent, sealed off from the outside world.

"My daughter is married to Jesus, like all the other nuns up there on the hill, and he's holding her captive!" Mrs. Reilly said to the clerk at the liquor store.

"Yeah, Christ the polygamist!" the clerk wise-cracked back, a nice guy, married with a son in fifth grade.

There were several pleasant clerks at El Cerrito Wine and Spirits. Mrs. Reilly got to know them all. One was working his way through college at U.C. Berkeley, such a bright boy. Why couldn't Edna find someone like HIM? But the clerk she saw most often turned out not to be a clerk at all but the owner of El Cerrito Wine and Spirits, Sidney Blumenthal. He was the one with the son in fifth grade, Ben. Ben had always been very bright but shy and bookish, his father said. Mrs. Reilly could sympathize. Her daughter Edna was the same way, an introvert. You never knew what was on her mind.

"Too bad," Sidney Blumenthal replied and shook his head. "Kids today. It's hard to understand them."

"I know it. My daughter is in a convent. What could she be doing in there all day?" Mrs. Reilly asked.

"I'm Jewish. I can't even imagine it. But kids today!" he said, again, and shook his head. "Who can understand it. When I was in fifth grade, I was a good student and I had a *job* after work!"

Mrs. Reilly had never had a job in her life, not even babysitting except for her own kids but at least she wasn't shy. She'd always been outgoing and enjoyed a little attention once in a while and she took pride in her appearance. It was December, getting chilly out. She was wearing her fox stole over her cashmere sweater and fitted wool jacket that day. It was the kind of fox with the jaw that could be clamped down onto any part of the rest of the dangling fox fur, to give different looks. Mrs. Reilly liked to get a little bit dressed up when she went out. And she always put on a *little lipstick*. You never knew who you'd meet. Sometimes, if she were in the mood, she'd wear a hat. Some had feathers. They were left over from the 30's and from the early 40's-- from before the war--but were still *perfectly good*.

Mr. Blumenthal never told her but he always hated that fox fur. He felt sorry for the fox. At least he liked Mrs. Reilly's hats, especially the ones with the little feathers, which she happened to be wearing that day. That feather, it was like a little antenna.

"I do love your hat," he exclaimed to Mrs. Reilly.

"Oh, thank you," she replied, distracted. She was trying to think of the name of a new cocktail she'd heard about. "It has lime and mint, I think," she said. Sid knew of several cocktails that required mint, and lime.

A few years went by. In 1952, or was it 1955? Hard for Mrs. Reilly to say but she bought something new, a TV! She enjoyed *I Love Lucy* and *The Taste of the Town* with Ed Sullivan. But her favorite TV personality was Edward R. Morrow. Every Friday on *Person to Person* Edward R. Morrow went to "visit" a different celebrity in his or her home via the miracle of television. You could see Edward R. Morrow in a dark TV studio, smoking cigarettes. You could see the glowing tip of his cigarette burning in the darkness. He preferred doing serious news, but he lit a cigarette and did what was required. Mrs. Reilly smoked along with him and had a Gin Gimlet. Something else that was new! She liked the taste of the Rose's Lime Juice.

Yes, she was enjoying her life right there in El Cerrito, a great little town just across The Bay from San Francisco. She could always go to San Francisco any time but why bother when you could stay at home and watch TV? Another of her favorite new shows was the *Dinah Shore Show*.

"See the USA, in your Chevrolet, America's the greatest land of all!"

Upbeat and blond, Dinah Shore sang this jingle and then threw a big kiss out to the TV audience, including Mrs. Reilly. MMM-wah! Nobody else was throwing a big kiss out to Mrs. Reilly, or even a little kiss.

Mrs. Reilly couldn't complain. She lived in a pleasant if modest three-bedroom ranch style house in El Cerrito, CA. It was a long walk to the bus stop but who needed to go anywhere when you had a TV? One day Mrs. Reilly got sick and tired of watching TV *alone* in her house, though. It was raining and she was sick and tired of taking the bus everywhere, sick and tired of having to carry her goddamn groceries home, especially in the rain. Her neighbors were all getting cars and she decided to get one, too.

"See the USA in your Chevrolet!"

She bought a Chevrolet and learned to drive it. Soon she could drive to the grocery store and to the liquor store, which would could come in handy especially in bad weather. The A & P grocery store and El Cerrito Wine and Spirits were both located in the new shopping mall, El Cerrito Center. It was a strip mall where you could park right in front. One fine day Mrs. Reilly actually drove her car to San Francisco, though, parked in a garage and went shopping. She came home with two big bags of form-fitting sweaters and big skirts with sparkly belts, like Dinah Shore's. Then she drove to the beauty parlor and got a new look. Instead of her usual straight, dark brown hair she had wavy blond hair, like Dinah Shore's!

Mr. Blumenthal was appalled. "Yellow hair, what next!" he said to himself. He thought her new blonde hair looked terrible but kept it to himself. He tried to think of something to say to her but was too appalled. Fortunately, Mrs. Reilly was distracted. She was trying to remember if she needed olives or cherries with her new drink recipe.

"What do you think, Sidney?" Sidney had been terrified to say what he really thought, but this relieved his mind.

"Six of one, half-dozen of the other. Depends." He wanted to say, "Why did you do that to your HAIR? It was fine the way it was!" At least she wasn't wearing that awful fox fur; but you have to look on the good side of things, Sid reminded himself, looking into Mrs. Reilly's eyes. She had such beautiful brown eyes. All he wanted to do was take her in his arms and smother her with kisses. He couldn't wait to see her again.

"Don't you like my hair, Sydney?" she wanted to say. "I did it for you." But she moved on. She still couldn't decide whether to get Maraschino Cherries or olives. But she could always come back, again and again. All she wanted to do was take him in her arms and smother him with kisses.

Chapter 3
"Claustrum"

The word *cloister* comes from the Latin *claustrum*, or *enclosure*. A claustrum or cloister can be a building attached to a church. It can be a covered walkway, maybe a walkway surrounding a courtyard or garden. A person in a religious order may lead a *claustral* life in an enclosed monastery--a cloister. Cloistered/contemplative orders of priests and monks include Benedictines and Dominicans and Trappists. Cloistered/contemplative orders of nuns include Carmelites and Dominicans. Among the lesser known orders is the Order of the Little Sisters of the Perpetual Rosary of Berkeley. It wasn't that far from El Cerrito, just up in the Berkeley Hills on the tippy top.

Here up on Grizzly Peak Edna got used to her new home and her new name. Here *Sister Mary Agatha* was content to live largely in silence behind her convent's cloistered walls. She loved being married to Christ. She welcomed poverty, chastity and obedience. The simplicity made life easier. She loved her long black habit and stiff white wimple, the feeling of it enclosing and encasing her body, a cross between a cardboard box and a cocoon. She loved her Mother Superior who made righteous decisions and cared deeply about the soul of each and every nun under her care and protection. In silence she found a special connection to God, and singing with the choir took her straight to heaven. But she loved her earthly work assignment, too. Each nun was given some kind of practical work.

Edna, now known as *Sister Mary Agatha*, worked in the bakery. It always smelled good! The convent had a menu of baked goods available wholesale. It helped the Little Sisters pay their bills, and with a portion left over for the Vatican. The menu of baked goods included:

St. Ambrose' Altar Bread:
Also known as "communion wafers." This was a top seller and provided reliable income. Saint Ambrose was known as a patron saint of bakers. As a baby he was visited by a swarm of bees who left little droplets of honey on his face and never stung him.

St. Hildegard's Cookies of Joy:
Inspired by Saint Hildegard's healthful and wholesome recipes to help with bad moods and strengthen nerves. She is known as a patron saint of nutritious foods and whole grain baked goods. They were not a big seller but made a dent in the bills.

ST. AGATHA'S Buns:
Inspired by St. Agatha of Sicily, *Sister Mary Agatha's* namesake, these sweet white buns were cut in half, placed in the oven flat side down, baked, covered in white icing, and dotted with a maraschino cherry to represent the nipples of St. Agatha's breasts, which were torn off by the Inquisition.

Sister Mary Agatha was enthralled with her new life. She didn't particularly like her new name but it was a small price to pay for her otherwise happy new life. She liked almost everything about her life in the convent, except her name. Saint Agatha was tortured on the rack, her breasts torn off during the Inquisition. Now she is a patron saint of breast cancer patients and breast cancer survivors. *Sister Mary Agatha* tried not to think about having her breasts torn off on the rack but was happy to pray every day for people who were having breast cancer treatments. Her mother was less than enthralled.

Mrs. Reilly had never approved of her daughter's marriage to Christ, not ever. She didn't enjoy the wedding and abhorred Edna's new name: *Sister Mary Agatha.*

"Sister Mary AGATHA, it sounds like Sister Mary AGONY. What the hell kind of a name is that!" Mrs. Reilly asked Mr. Blumenthal.

"Beats me! Get it? *Agony*--beats me! Hah!"

"Hah! That's a good one!" Mrs. Reilly said. "But seriously. This Saint Agatha of Sicily, I looked it up in end encyclopedia. She was *Sicilian.* We're not even Italian. My husband was Irish and I was English, a *Holmes.*"

"Like Sherlock Holmes! Go figure. Get it? Go figure? Sherlock Holmes? Hah!"

"Sid, you are such a card!"

"And look on the good side, that name Agatha, it reminds me of AGATHA Christy. She was a big success with her mysteries. Am I right?"

"Of course." Mrs. Reilly started to cry.

"But in all seriousness," Mr. Blumenthal said sympathetically, patting her hand helplessly. "Some things make no sense. My son loves POETRY. We were from Poland. If he had to be *arty*, he could at least play the piano. Chopin was Polish! I think that's where you get that Polonaise thing from, right, from Poland?" Then he started to cry, too.

Eleanora reached over and squeezed Sidney's hand, just for a second.

"My son, if he had to be an *artsy* poet, I should have called him Arthur. His nickname could have been *Arty*. Get it? Arty the Poet!" He tried to stop crying and be cheerful.

"Oh, Sid. Poets are wonderful. I named Edna after a poet!"

"No kidding!"

"No. I named her after Edna St. Vincent Millay. I was HOPING she'd be a poet one day."

"Really?"

"Would I kid you? No. I used to read poetry to her before she was born, and even during the war. It helped me get through the War, know what I mean?"

"I understand. We were lucky. Most of my people were Polish, Polish Jews. Thank God most of them were already gone, everyone we knew of."

"Thank God," Mrs. Reilly said, heart to heart.

Meanwhile back in the convent, *Sister Mary Agatha* prayed every night to St. Agatha of Sicily and to Saint Mary the Blessed Mother to intercede with God and show her the right path through life. Everything was fine. The praying and the singing and the baking, it all worked out. The bills were paid with a little left over for the Vatican.

Chapter 4
"1955"

Mrs. Reilly had always liked the name EDNA. It was a well-balanced name: two consonants and two vowels. It was easy to pronounce, ED-NA. It had a ring to it. It was a perfect name. Now she had a new name. Like everyone else, her first name would be *Mary* in honor of the Blessed Mother. Her second name would be in honor of an extra saint, in Edna's case that was St. Agatha. But why?

The next day Mrs. Reilly went back to the Public Library and looked up Saint Edna, again in different encyclopedias. Maybe she missed something the first time. Aha! Yes, a woman named *Edna* (also spelled "Edaene" or "Etaoin") was canonized as "St. Modwenna" in the 9th century, way before modern record keeping. Mother Superior was wrong. Hah! There <u>was</u> a Saint Edna. "That's it," Mrs. Reilly said to herself later that night after she'd had a few more cocktails. "I've had it." She tried to call Mother Superior and tell her what she'd learned about St. Edna but nobody answered. She'd tried frequently to call over the years, mostly after she'd had a few cocktails, but it never worked. Nobody answered the phone after 5pm.

"What if it were an emergency?" Mrs. Reilly asked Mr. Blumenthal at the liquor store. "And that name, SISTER AGATHA, I objected to that name from Day One," she went on. She couldn't get it out of her mind. "AGATHA, it sounds like AGONY! What the hell! My daughter is Sister Mary AGONY—named after Saint AGONY!"

"Go figure!" Sid Blumenthal said as kindly as a man could possibly say the words, from behind the counter, which greatly endeared him to Mrs. Reilly. Sometimes all you need is a kind word.

"That damned Mother Superior disrespected the name EDNA," Mrs. Reilly went on."

"You, her mother, they never respected YOU!" Sidney asserted. "A mother should be respected!"

Mrs. Eleanora Holmes Reilly appreciated Mr. Sidney Blumenthal's support. Her suspicions were confirmed, her suspicions about Mother Superior.

"I only got to talk to that Mother Superior once since my daughter *took her veil.* But I asked her, 'where'd you get that name *Sister Mary Agatha?* What's wrong with *Sister Mary EDNA?*' And that damned Mother Superior tried to tell me there was no *Saint Edna.* There *was* a Saint EDNA. I looked it up in an encyclopedia," she said to Sidney Blumenthal as he rang up her vodka and olives stuffed with pimento.

"I don't know," Sidney confessed, starting to feel tired. "I've never been a religious person but I don't think we have saints in the Jewish faith. I could be wrong. But as far as I know we just have rabbis."

"I see," she said, suddenly distracted. She looked around the store, as if she'd never seen it before. "Whatever happened to that nice young fellow who used to work here, the one with the crew cut. Jimmy, was that his name?"

"That nice young fellow Jimmy is going off to the University of Hawaii, to study *surfing.* Surfing, I ask you! Isn't *that* something?"

"That is something. Whoever heard of studying surfing in college? Well, times change and time flies, that's for sure."

"You said it. My son Ben is going to college this year!"

"I'm shocked!" Mrs. Reilly replied. "Your BEN is going to college, already!"

"Yes! He's going to study POETRY. Poetry, where will it get us? I ask you!"

"I enjoy poetry sometimes. But for a young man? He's got to support a family one day."

"Not to worry! At the rate he's going he'll never have one. Go figure."

It was 1955. For ten years Edna Reilly (AKA *Sister Mary Agatha*) remained in the convent, quite happily. But after ten years she began to wonder about the outside world. She began to wonder what she was doing there. And then came rushing back to her, all the reasons

12

why she went into the convent in the first place, the very hell of it. 1942, the war, the death, and the sad cigarette smoke in her mother's house. The air up on top of Holy Hill was so clean and pure but maybe ten years of clean air was enough.

Sister Mary Agatha prayed to the Blessed Mother and to St. Agatha to intercede for her with God. "I don't mean to cause any trouble, but please get me out of here. I'd like to go out into the world again. If you have any ideas please give me a sign. Just a word or two, even a nod would be good, or an omen. Omens are good. Thank you. Your devoted servant, Sister Mary Agatha."

For another year or two nothing happened. But one day out of the blue Sister Mary Agatha heard a voice, a deep operatic basso profundo voice. It sounded like the Voice of God.

"Hello?" said the Voice of God. "Hello? Anyone at home?"

"God, is it you?"

"It is I, the Voice of God!" the voice boomed.

"*The Voice of God*--is that the same as *God?*"

"*The Voice of God*--is that the same as *God?*"

"Yes," the Voice of God replied, "one and the same, audible and inaudible. I have many voices but today I speak in the voice of Paul Robeson, *basso baritone*, the deepest of all vocal ranges. Paul Robeson, who is African-American, is best known in America for singing 'Ole Man River,' but he's off in Moscow now singing 'The International'--*in Russian*. I think he might be a *communist;* but he has his reasons for what he does. I've tried to help him. And what may I do for YOU today, my child?"

"Call me crazy but I'm thinking of leaving the convent," said and waited for the Voice of God to talk her out of it. But no.

"Very well," said the Voice of God. "For over ten long years you have been my trusted servant here with the Little Sisters. You have been a good baker. You have prayed silently and sincerely. You have sung well with the choir. In you I am well pleased. After ten years you'd like to emerge into the outside world. Who could blame you? The question is: where in the outside world would you like to go?"

"I have no idea. I've been here for so long."

"Well, that is a problem. If you don't have an exit strategy, how can I help you get where you want to go?"

"Can't you find one for me? Can't you just get me out of here?"

"Yes, my child, of course I can. But it's your voyage, not mine. And besides, it's not the destination; it's the journey. You need to come up with your *own* game plan. I'll help you but you must bear the brunt. Your path will require great sacrifice, total devotion. Are you ready to take Step #1?"

"Yes."

"Very well. Step #1 requires that you begin to think for yourself and quit letting Mother Superior run your life. Can you handle it?"

"Yes."

"Very well. I'll give you a few clues. Great obstacles must be overcome and enemies smote. Listen closely."

"I'm listening."

"Sister Mary Agatha, I the Voice of God want you to follow your bliss."

"My bliss?"

"Yes, your bliss. My trusted servant Joseph Campbell will explain this concept on Public Television at a later date. But this channel does not yet exist. In fact, you have never seen a television, have you?"

"Television, no, God."

"Of course not. You've been on another planet, hiding out in that god-forsaken convent. You must be sick of the view from Grizzly Peak by now!"

"Well, yes. You see there's this fog bank. We should have a nice view of San Francisco Bay but it's relentless. On a good day we can see the Rose Garden or the rooftops on Holy Hill."

"Ah, the Protestants. Yes, I know. But can you imagine walking around the Rose Garden or going into a library in one of the Protestant seminaries on Holy Hill? They're most welcoming and you could do all the reading you wanted! You could search your soul, go to Timbuktu, or discover your bliss walking around Lake Merritt in Oakland. Or go to Hollywood. Find your bliss, EDNA. Think of it as my First Commandment, "Follow Your Bliss.""

"Bliss, in this world of sorrows?"

14

"Have another world in mind? Please, my child. Tell me your hopes and dreams. Have any?"

"World Peace?"

"World Peace, it's too *vague*. The problem is HOW to achieve World Peace, that's what we want to know. It's never been done on Earth, not for long. If you figure it out let us know. My trusted servant Paul Robeson is traveling all over the world, trying to figure it out."

She had no specifics for achieving World Peace but God did not give up on her. God just gave her more time to think about it, a couple of years, two at tops.

Chapter 5
"1957"

In 1957 Sister Mary Agatha was still in the convent. She'd been there for twelve years by this time. Things were starting to get on her nerves. She began to dislike her white wimple for some reason. And the large crucifix around her neck seemed to pull her closer to the ground, inviting scoliosis and early death. She prayed repeatedly to St. Agatha of Sicily and to the Blessed Mother to intercede with God. They ignored her. She then tried praying directly to God. Nothing, nada. She began to have *resentments* and resentments build up.

"Well, *Sister Mary Agatha*," the Voice of God boomed out again at long last, "any plan for BLISS? Anything blissful on the horizon?"

"No, God."

"Too bad. Or as they say in Russian—but never mind. My child, what about your bliss? Any thoughts at all?"

"No, nothing came to me."

"Too bad. I was afraid of that. Are you ready to hear my proposal for Step #1 of your journey? It's actually more of a command. Let's call it a Commandment—the First Commandment. OK?"

"OK!"

"Very well, listen and obey."

"Yes, yes!"

"The path ahead will be steep and perilous. Step #1 of my plan will require you to go back home and move in with your mother."

"With my mother!"

"I told you the path would be steep and perilous."

"I see what you mean." She didn't know what she wanted. But she knew what she didn't want; she didn't want to move back in with her mother. "That would not be blissful at all."

"You may take it or you may leave it. We'd find something else for you in time but if you'd rather just stay in the convent, have a nice life in the convent," the Voice of God said and faded away.

"God, wait! Please come back! I'll do it. I'll do it!"

"Well, finally!" the Voice of God said, at the last second. "Think of it as just Step #1, one small step for you, but one large step for humanity. A journey of a thousand miles begins with one step. Ready to face more truisms?"

"Yes," Sister Mary Agatha was ready.

Chapter 6
"Mid-Life Crisis"

Mr. Blumenthal was a liberal. Mrs. Reilly had never thought about politics, never formed any opinions about anything too much outside El Cerrito. But she was a good person. "I like Ike," she said, over and over. She was a Democrat, but she liked Ike. And she hated "to see those kids in Little Rock being insulted and taunted, just for trying to go to school," she said to Mr. Blumenthal at the liquor store.

"Me, too!" he agreed. "Eisenhower had to call out the National Guard. It's on the TV news every night. What a sin!" Sid Blumenthal said.

"A sin and a shame," Mrs. Reilly agreed. "It's a sin how they're treating those kids." Her hair was nice and light and bright. She just had it colored and styled.

"And I wish you'd quit dying your hair BLONDE," Sidney Blumenthal wanted to say in reply. "It reminds me of my wife's hair." But he didn't say that. He tried to make the point indirectly. "I recently heard a rumor. I know it's strange, but I heard that BLONDE Dinah Shore was actually BLACK. Isn't that interesting? Who cares what race she is or if she dyes her hair? She would look just as beautiful with black or brown hair—kinky, curly or straight. Don't you agree?"

"Absolutely," Mrs. Reilly agreed. She didn't get the hint; he liked her hair better the way it was, naturally brown. But she was distracted. "Is Dinah Shore really black? Who said that?"

He couldn't recall. It's what someone said.

In El Cerrito, everything was peaceful and everyone was nice. The public schools were nice. Everyone was welcome. Gasoline was still 25 cents a gallon, and Mrs. Reilly still had her same Chevrolet. Sometimes she'd take herself on a nice drive down to the Berkeley Marina and walk out on the fishing pier. Sometimes she'd drive up into the Berkeley Hills to take a look at Edna's convent, just take a little look-see. She never stopped in; she wasn't permitted. But wherever she went she always stopped in at El Cerrito Wine and Spirits on her way home.

When she walked in that evening, Sidney Blumenthal was smoking a cigarette at the check-out counter and reading the newspaper, all alone.

"All alone, Sidney?"

"Yep, since Ben and Jimmy left for college I'm a one-man band here. But at least I don't have to go outside to smoke a cigarette," he mentioned while he reached for her favorite brand of cigarettes and vodka. "Ben and Jimmy always hated it when I smoked. My wife hates it when I smoke!"

"My daughter always hated it when I smoked; but she's still in that damned convent," Mrs. Reilly called out, walking off to the vodka section of the store, bringing it back to the counter. "At least with Edna in the convent I can smoke all I want at home. I have my house ALL TO MYSELF!" (Hint, Hint!)

It was hard to say how it started that evening. Mr. Blumenthal put Mrs. Reilly's purchases into a paper bag and handed it to her. Mrs. Reilly reached out and looked up. Their eyes locked. Years of repressed affection did it. Mrs. Reilly took her treasures and headed for the exit door. Mr. Blumenthal was right behind her. He stopped only to turn out the lights and lock the door. The evening proved to be a little awkward.

"I guess I'm out of practice," Mrs. Reilly laughed, sipping her Gin Gimlet.

"You're not the only one. My wife quit having anything to do with me years ago. Now my son's off in college. Nobody cares!"

"I care, Sidney," Mrs. Reilly said. "You're my best friend!"

"You're my only friend, Eleanora," Mr. Blumenthal said. "Everyone else just pretends."

The next day things went much better. And the day after that and the day after that.

"Heaven must have sent you!" Mr. Blumenthal said.

"Heaven must have sent YOU!" Mrs. Reilly said. "I've been waiting for you for years!"

19

"Me, too! My wife is going to take me to the cleaners. And my son is still in college, studying poetry in OHIO. I'm footing the bill-- and paying extra for out-of-state tuition!"

"I know, my love," Mrs. Reilly said. "You're caught between a rock and a hard place. But let's blow this joint!"

Maybe they both suffered from Mid-Life Crisis, or maybe just Middle Age Spread. They were both nominally a little overweight and flabby here and there but you could always turn out the lights. And there were wonderful creams for women and you could just use your imagination and have a lovely time, Mrs. Reilly said, happily. Mr. Blumenthal agreed. They hadn't invented Viagra yet, but neither of them cared. It was true love. They just got used to it. It felt like heaven. They felt like they were going somewhere together, somewhere fun! Mr. Blumenthal might have been going crazy, he said, but he never went home again. He never went back to his wife, and he didn't even try to make up an excuse for where he'd gone or what he was doing. He just stopped talking to his wife, or tried to.

Mrs. Blumenthal didn't know where her husband was at night any more, but she knew where to find him during the day, working at the liquor store.

"This is MY store, Sidney. It's in MY name," she reminded him. "I just want you to think about that before you go too far with this, this THING, whatever it is."

One evening Sidney's now *estranged* wife drove all over town, looking for him. But he'd already locked up the liquor store, gone to Mrs. Reilly's house and parked his car in her garage--so his wife couldn't see it.

A few days later, Eleanora and Sidney wanted to go outside but they were too afraid of MRS. Blumenthal. Trapped inside, the two love birds used their imaginations and decided to go on a honeymoon even though they weren't married. They packed some clothes, got into Mrs. Reilly's car, and drove till they got tired of driving. When they got tired, they stopped at a motel. The next day when they got tired, they stopped at a motel in Lake Havisu City, Arizona.

20

"The entire London Bridge will be here one day," the motel clerk said. "They're bringing it in pieces--from London! They're going to build it back up, right here, piece by piece."

"That's incredible," Sid said. "What an effort!"

"See what I mean?" Eleanora said later in their room, cozy together. "Imagination can lead to great things! Today, empty space. Tomorrow the London Bridge could be right next door!"

"You have a magnificent imagination," Sidney said, stroking the side of her face. "It's one of the many things I cherish about you."

They went out for burgers. The love birds gazed into each other's eyes, and then they went back to their motel. It was a nice motel. And it was FOR SALE!

"Sidney, what if we bought this place?"

"Oh, we could never do that. My wife's going to have a fit when she finds out where I am. She'll take me to the cleaners. And the liquor store is in her name. We haven't been very smart about this."

"Well, don't worry about her. She'll have plenty of money. And we have each other!"

Mrs. Reilly and Mr. Blumenthal did look into buying the motel but it turned out to be more expensive than they ever imagined. The London Bridge was coming to Lake Havisu very soon, after all. Real estate was going up. Oh well. Darn. Gosh darn it all.

"We'll dream up a better idea tomorrow," Mrs. Reilly said.

"I have no doubt," Mr. Blumenthal said. "But now I guess I'd better go back to El Cerrito and start filing for divorce."

"Oh, Sidney," Mrs. Reilly said. "That is music to my ears. We'll face the music together!"

She bought a special fun hat for the return trip, a straw hat with built-in sunglasses. And off they went, back to El Cerrito, right back to her house. Mr. Blumenthal's car was still safe and sound in the garage.

"We're in big trouble now," Mr. Blumenthal said, after he'd been to visit his lawyer.

"I figured that much. Care for a cocktail?" Mrs. Reilly said.

"Oh, I never drink. You know that, sweetie. But I'd love a cup of tea and a good snuggle!"

Mrs. Reilly was only too happy to oblige.

Over breakfast the next morning the Love Birds tried to come up with some new ideas. What to do. What to do. Mr. Blumenthal still had to help his son get through college. One day he'd have alimony to pay, too.

"You don't know," Mrs. Reilly said. "Maybe she'll have to pay YOU alimony. It's her liquor store, right?"

"I don't think it works that way, sweetie." He didn't know how these things worked. He'd never been divorced. But Mrs. Reilly had a few ideas.

"I know! We can sell my house!"

"But this is a terrible idea!" Mr. Blumenthal said. "What would people say? They'll say that I dumped my wife and ran off with a young beauty, and that I'm using you for your house! Can you imagine the humiliation? I couldn't stand it. What would my son say?"

Sometimes beauty is in the eye of the beholder. Mr. Blumenthal had perhaps been foolish, unwise. But, as he tried to explain it to his lawyer, his wife had frozen them out of their bedroom years ago and now he'd finally found someone who cared.

"I've finally found true love. She's beautiful and she loves me. No one should begrudge me that."

"No one begrudges you, Sid. But it's gonna cost you, that's all. And that Mrs. Reilly of yours is going to be named your hot tamale. Not much we can do with that. But we'll do the best we can."

After his second meeting with his lawyer, Mr. Blumenthal returned with a realization. Yes, the future would have a few bumps in the road. But he was heading out anyway, with his true love.

"I don't know about you, Eleanora, but I feel like going back to Lake Havisu City!" he said, feeling positive, upbeat, energetic. "There's no stopping us now!"

"Sidney, that is thrilling!" she exclaimed.

"This time we can take my car," he suggested. "We went in your car last time."

"Deal!" she said.

They figured things out together, step by step. The next day Mr. Blumenthal put their suitcases in the car and slipped behind the driver's seat. Mrs. Reilly was in her boudoir taking a minute to put on her straw hat with the built-in sunglasses, and a little lipstick. She was just standing there in the bathroom smiling at her lips in the mirror when the phone rang. It was EDNA. She'd been calling and calling.

"Where have you been, Mom? I've called you so often!"

"Oh. Edna, I've called you a thousand times over the years, too!"

"But I mean this week. I've been calling you this week. You're never home."

"Oh, I've been doing this and that with a friend."

"Mom," Edna said, and then just spit it out. "Mom, would it be OK to stay in the house for a while? I'm leaving the convent."

"Oh, Edna. I can't believe it! I can't believe it!" Mrs. Reilly screamed. "My baby is coming back! Oh my God, this is great news!" But then she stopped. Sidney was out in the car waiting for her. Now what? She didn't know what to think. She couldn't think. "Can you call me back in five minutes?"

"Sure, Mom. Thanks."

Edna's period of transition after her exclaustration had been moving along faster than she'd anticipated. It took her a while to come to the full realization that she would really be leaving and moving back in with her mother. And Eleanora, in a state of shock, didn't know what to say and Sidney who was waiting out in the car. After he got tired of waiting for her to put on her lipstick and grab her hat and pocketbook, he turned off the engine and trudged back in. A few hours later he got back in his car and drove to Arizona, alone. He wasn't angry. He just wasn't ready to meet Edna. And Edna was not ready to meet HIM. She didn't even know he existed. The separation would only be temporary and probably for the best, the love birds agreed, at least until his divorce was finalized. Off he went, Sidney Blumenthal, driving off to Lake Havisu City alone.

Mrs. Reilly hoped she'd hear from him again but you never know. Life has a way of getting you in trouble, ruining some of your most glorious hopes and dreams. She hoped for the best. And her baby

23

was coming home! She couldn't NOT be there, not after so many years. She immediately opened all the windows so Edna wouldn't smell the cigarette smoke. And then she sat down to make herself a nice drinky-poo and do a little thinking.

Chapter 7
"Claustrophobia"

Exclaustration is the process by which nuns who want to be released from their Final Vows and stay in good standing with The Church may do so. It's based on the "Codex Luris Canonici," Canon Law. *Exclaustration* must be approved by Church Officials and there must be a good reason. It was hard for Sister Mary Agatha to say what her reason was. It was time to go, that was the reason, time to leave the claustrum. And the process includes a period of transition.

Once Sister Mary Agatha had permission to leave and the transitional period was over, she was a free woman again! She was *Edna* again. It was the first time in twelve years that Edna had stepped outside the convent not wearing a habit. Edna was 29. She looked every minute of 40. Mrs. Reilly picked her up in her Chevrolet and tried not to stare at Edna's hair. It was chopped off in little clumps, like the women in Paris who had Nazi lovers during the War and were jeered at by crowds. But that wasn't important. Her baby was back, that's what was important. Edna and her Mom hugged and cried, got in the car, and away they went.

"My baby's back! My baby's back!" Mrs. Reilly exclaimed, lighting a cigarette at a red light.

"Yes, I'm back. I can't believe it! But, Mom, could you please open the window?"

Mrs. Reilly readily obliged, opening the window a tiny crack, blowing smoke out as she drove, holding onto the steering wheel with her right hand while she flicked ashes out into the world with her left. Her left hand was now decorated with a new *engagement ring* but Edna didn't notice the ring, just the smoke. That smoke, Edna had almost forgotten it. She started to feel slightly nauseous. Claustrophobia (fear of the claustrum) started to set in.

They finally arrived in the neighborhood. It looked very different from the way it looked in 1947. When Edna left for the convent people were out strolling babies, old people were out taking health walks, *housewives* were out hanging laundry in their backyards. "Where are all the neighbors?" Edna asked. Sad to say but some of the older neighbors had passed away, some mothers went back to work, and everyone had washing machines and cars and TV's and you just never saw them anymore. Edna's mother thought some new people might have moved in across the street. She never met them but it didn't matter. Edna was back. That's what mattered. "My baby's back! My baby's back!" Mrs. Reilly rejoiced again as she pulled her Chevrolet into the garage.

Inside the house, Edna walked down the old familiar hallway to her old bedroom. The wall paper was the same, a tropical leafy pattern. The beige carpet was still soft under her feet. Her old bedroom looked different now, like a hotel room. She sat down on the bed and prayed for guidance.

While her daughter was busy praying, Mrs. Reilly got busy making a pitcher of cocktails. She got out the fizzy water, ice, vodka and Maraschino cherries, mixed everything up and sat two frosty glasses down on cocktail napkins that read "HAPPY NEW YEAR!" left over from a quiet New Year's Eve. Edna wouldn't care for a cocktail, thanks. She'd never had one. She went into the convent at age 18. The only alcohol she ever had was a single sip of wine at communion. Edna just wanted a lovely glass of water. Water would be wonderful, thank you.

After the "cocktail *hour*" Mrs. Reilly got out packages of roasted sliced chicken and potato salad from the deli and put everything on her best china. As they enjoyed their dinner, Mrs. Reilly and Edna started to get reacquainted. Mrs. Reilly was so happy. All she wanted to do was welcome her daughter back home and help her enter a new phase in her life.

"And I'm taking you to my beauty salon tomorrow. My treat! We'll get you a new hair style for starters. Did you cut it yourself?" Mrs. Reilly tried to be tactful.

"I did," Edna said, and started to cry.

"Oh, honey," Mrs. Reilly said, and got up and hugged her.

They could always go to the beauty shop another day. In the meantime, Mrs. Reilly and Edna sat and cried together. It had been a long separation. After they stopped crying, they each blew their noses and sat in silence for a few minutes. Edna was used to silence. Mrs. Reilly was used to radio and TV. Somehow, they got through the day, through lunch and dinner. And then it was 7:30pm. Any minute the phone would ring. Mr. Blumenthal would be calling from Lake Havisu City. Mrs. Reilly wasn't sure what to say about HIM to Edna; and so she said little.

"I have a friend," she said, finally.

"A friend?"

"Yes, a companion type of friend."

"That's nice, Mom. Who is she?"

"He's a HE. His name is Sidney."

"Oh. Why don't you invite him over?"

"He's in Arizona, exploring business possibilities."

"Oh," Edna said and dropped the subject.

Just then the phone rang. It was *him*. Mrs. Reilly dashed down the hall to pick up the call on the extension phone in her room. It was her mother's *friend*. More would be revealed later.

The next morning although Mrs. Reilly didn't feel very well, she made some scrambled eggs. And although she had a headache, she was chatty. Edna was used to silence at breakfast, or maybe a spiritual reading. "You know, it's hard being single. Believe me, I know," Edna's mother chatted on, adding a little salt and pepper to the scrambled eggs. Edna didn't miss the convent, but she did miss breakfast at the convent, the long tables and the long silences. She missed her Sisters. She never expected to miss Mother Superior, but she did.

"More coffee?" Mrs. Reilly offered.

"No thanks," Edna replied. "I think I'll just take a shower."

In the bathroom, she knew it was probably a sin to stare at herself in the mirror but she couldn't help it. Edna faced her reflection. What a shock! Her red curly hair was still there, starting to grow out from its stubs. Her blue eyes were still blue, but they were by now slightly framed by small crows' feet. No wonder they had no mirrors in the convent! Edna looked in the mirror and found a stranger, and so did Edna's mother. It was a big adjustment for both of them. And Edna had never seen a television!

"TV!" Edna said later that evening. "Wow!"

27

"Hey, get with the times!" her Mom chirped, turning on the TV.

Edna was fascinated. It was 1957 almost 1958. Television was still in its infancy, or at least its childhood. Mrs. Reilly remembered when Edna was an infant, the most perfect little dream of a girl in the world. She'd been gone a long time but now she was back just in time to watch the *Ed Sullivan Show*. "Elvis the Pelvis" was going to be on! "Elvis the Pelvis," they call him, Mrs. Reilly explained to her daughter, "but all they show is from the shoulders up."

And there he was in all his glory, Elvis Presley, from his shoulders to the top of his head. Elvis was considered to be lewd and was x-rated by the censors, even though he was fully dressed, including jacket and necktie. Edna was bewildered.

"Oh," Edna's mother said. "Elvis is the best, the King! Have a beer?"

"No thanks, Mom," Edna replied.

"Here, this one is already open. Have half with me," she said, handing her a cup of beer. "Relax!" She didn't know what else to say to her daughter. "Ike is still in charge. There's nothing to worry about. I like Ike! That's what we say."

Edna wasn't sure if she liked Ike or not, or if she liked TV or not. She liked silence. She liked singing with the choir. She liked baking and she loved her Sisters. Mrs. Reilly liked Sidney. She liked watching TV with Sidney in the evenings. She was afraid to tell Edna about Sidney, about how much she cared for Sidney, about how much she missed him. Good thing he was in Lake Havisu City, Mrs. Reilly reminded herself. Edna needed a period of adjustment. No point in pushing things. And she didn't know how to tell Edna how much she'd missed *her* and how happy she was to have her back. But her daughter had been a nun for almost twelve years. How could she ever explain the fact that a married man was waiting for her in a motel in Lake Havisu City, Arizona? How could she?

Every night at 7:30 Mr. Blumenthal called, religiously. Mrs. Reilly had a lovely pink Princess Phone with a long extension cord in her bedroom. She could even take into the private bathroom of her master suite for private talks. Edna knew very well that this must be her mother's new boyfriend, the one who was in Arizona on business. Who else could she be talking to every evening at 7:30 in secret? "Oh, it's a friend," Mrs. Reilly said. Then another thought crossed Edna's mind: would her mother ever get married again? She wondered. But this was not very likely. Edna's mother was 52 years old and had (in Edna's experience) lived in that house forever, mostly all alone. But it was 1958. Life was changing.

In 1958 a newly recognized tribe of Native Americans, the Lumbee, defeated the KKK in a battle in North Carolina. Few people in El Cerrito had heard about the Battle of Lumbee. Most people knew that the USSR launched Sputnik III, though, and that Elvis Presley was drafted into the US Army. And there was a recession going on, the Great Recession of 1958, and Dwight Eisenhower was still President. Everyone knew that, too. "I like Ike!" Mrs. Reilly re-affirmed. "He got us through the war. He'll get us out of this mess, too."

The Great Recession of 1958 was wide-spread but didn't last *too* long. Still there were problems with labor and strikes. In 1959 there would be more problems but in 1958 people still hoped for a better future with more labor-saving devices and bigger cars with bigger tail fins, just as soon as the steel workers strike was over. Mrs. Reilly mixed up another pitcher of cocktails and poured some into a coffee cup. Then she smoked a cigarette in her bedroom with the window cracked open one inch. She had a lot to think about.

Chapter 8
"I Found My Thrill, On Blueberry Hill"

For almost twelve years Edna had lived in a state of voluntary poverty, as unpaid labor. She hadn't minded. She was doing God's work but that was then. Now it was time for Edna to look for a paying job. Unfortunately, it was a bad time to be job hunting. There was a recession going on.

Day after day Edna walked around El Cerrito in search of a job. Sorry not hiring. Sorry don't need anyone. She prayed, sang hymns and read inspirational literature. Nothing worked. And if God had some secret plan for Edna, it was not apparent. God did not fill her soul with inspiration and/or direction. But her mother had a few ideas.

"Get a government job," Mrs. Reilly suggested. "What about a government job? Government jobs are the best because they can't fire you."

"I wasn't fired, Mom!" Edna reminded her. "I left the convent of my own free will."

Edna left her convent on good terms and could always go back. But she didn't want to go back! That morning she ventured into a new place, El Cerrito Plaza. It was a *shopping center.* Time was, people took the bus to a store, or walked. Now people had cars and drove them to *shopping centers* where they could park right in front of any store.

Edna walked to the El Cerrito Plaza shopping center. It wasn't THAT far. The first shop was El Cerrito Wine and Spirits. They had a "HELP WANTED, Full-Time" sign in the window but she decided to skip that one. She walked from shop to shop, stopping to inquire about employment. She finally got to the very last shop at the end of the plaza. Good thing it was the end because she was getting tired. But here at the end of the shopping plaza was a little place that smelled like blueberries, a bakery! Music was piped out onto the sidewalk in front, a song by Fats Domino. It was one of his greatest Top Hits called "Blueberry Hill." It was the Blueberry Hill Bakery.

Edna entered and sat on a stool at the counter. She hadn't sat on a stool at a counter since she was in high school. It felt strange, but she was tired and needed to sit down. A kindly server immediately gave her a glass of water and invited her to look at the menu on the chalkboard in front of her. It was a large chalkboard with an extensive menu. There were blueberry muffins, blueberry scones, blueberry parfait, and blueberry donuts, etc.

"I am sorry but I can't decide what to order," Edna confessed to the kindly server. "Is it better to order a muffin or a donut?"

"I'd go with a donut," she said. "They're the best value but you can't go wrong here. I wouldn't steer you wrong, sister. It's all good."

The server called her "sister." It made Edna feel at home again. Instead of a white wimple and black veil the woman was wearing a little cap shaped like a large blueberry. Under the blueberry was a blue hair net. Edna opted for a blueberry donut. She'd never had a blueberry donut, she mentioned, staring down at her hands, trying to avoid eye contact, which she'd been trained to do in the convent. But THIS was the beginning of her new life outside the convent, she told the server. Edna broke out! She spoke to a person, a complete stranger wearing a plastic blueberry on her head. She told the stranger about leaving her convent and about walking around the plaza looking for a job. And the stranger was nice!

"We have a job opening!" she said. "It's just part-time. But we need someone to work at the counter and help with baking. I don't suppose you've ever done any baking?"

"Yes!" Edna said, "Yes, I have baked, in the convent!"

"Unbelievable!" the server said. "This is a real God-send!"

The next day Edna had a JOB at the Blueberry Hill Bakery! They'd just had to let someone go. Now they needed someone who could BAKE and wait on customers. And they needed someone who was *honest*. They'd had a few problems with things disappearing lately, out of the till and through the front door. Nothing serious, but it had gotten worse since the Recession started, the Manager explained.

This job was just part-time but here she was, wearing a little cap that looked like a big blueberry with a blue hairnet underneath. Most people didn't look that good in a hairnet. Edna didn't. But you have to wear one if you're serving baked goods to the public--in case a hair falls onto a plate or into a little white waxed paper bag. Edna didn't look good but she hadn't looked that good in a white wimple and black habit either. But looks had nothing to do with it. Edna was here to work. Sometimes she worked at the counter serving customers. Sometimes she worked in the back room, baking scones, bread, muffins, cake and/or donuts. The owner of Blueberry Hill Bakery was well pleased. God was well pleased. Edna was happy but Edna's mother was not.

Mrs. Reilly was afraid that Edna would wander down to the other end of the shopping center to the El Cerrito Wine and Spirits, and apply for that *full-time* job. Since Mr. Blumenthal went to Florida, Mrs. Reilly drove by the liquor store now and then, hoping to pick up a little bottle of something but she had to drive on to the next liquor store. MRS. BLUMENTHAL was always there. She could see her through the window right there at the cash register. And the "HELP WANTED, full-time" sign was still up. Nobody could stand to work there with her for long. At least Edna was not a drinker. She wouldn't be dropping in to pick up booze and meet Sidney's (estranged) WIFE. If Edna happened to get chummy with her, Mrs. Blumenthal would have a field day during the divorce!

"Good morning, sweetie," Edna's mother said weakly, early the next morning. She hadn't slept well and was having a cup of coffee with a wee little shot of whiskey. It eased the symptoms of *anything*. She took a nice big gulp.

"Care for a blueberry donut, Mom?" Edna was getting a white waxed-paper bag out of the refrigerator. They let Edna take day-old treats home, no charge.

"No thanks, maybe later."

Mrs. Reilly picked up her coffee, toddled back to her bedroom, cracked open the window and lit a cigarette. "Why can't she get a Federal Government job, maybe in some nice National Park like the Grand Canyon?" she asked herself, taking a deep inhale of nicotine, exhaling out the window. "Or what about a state job, in Sacramento? It's nice in Sacramento."

Edna continued baking and waiting on customers at Blueberry Hill Bakery. Everything was moving so FAST. It was 1958. There were so many CARS! Where was everyone going? Edna continued her prayers and meditations regularly. She used to feel God's presence in the convent every day in the silence. But not *here*.

Chapter 9
"A Real God Send"

Edna went to work that morning on the early shift and started baking. Then it was her turn to wait on customers. After the morning rush was over Edna used the free time to polish things up, make them shiny and bright. Oops, out of coffee! She was just pouring some water into the big coffee urn as she heard Fats Domino singing, "I found my thrill, on Blueberry Hill..." It was a new customer.

"I'll be right with you!" Edna called out. She couldn't turn around because she was busy pouring water into the coffee urn.

"OK!" a cheerful male voice called back.

Edna poured all the water into the urn, pushed the ON button and turned around to find a man wearing a brown robe and a crucifix around his neck. Edna was started. She wasn't used to seeing men in brown robes, a Franciscan friar? She wasn't sure. He was maybe 65 with a mop of gray hair.

"Good morning!" he chirped.

"Good morning, father," she replied, eyes cast down again, as she'd been trained in the convent.

"Oh, I'm not a FATHER," he smiled. "I'm a BROTHER. Brother Flynn, pleased to meet you!"

"Pleased to meet you," Edna replied, nervously. She didn't know why she was so nervous. She just wasn't expecting a "religious."

"And pleased to meet you." He studied the Specials of the Day on the chalkboard menu up on the wall in front of him.

"May I take your order?" Edna asked.

"Just coffee, thanks," he replied, getting out his *San Francisco Chronicle* from his brief case. "Did you do the Jumble today?" he asked cheerfully.

"The Jumble?"

"Yes, the Jumble, the puzzle."

He started working on his puzzle and Edna buzzed around, cleaning and polishing and staying busy while the coffee brewed.

"Water?"

"Yes, thank you," he smiled.

She brought him a glass of water and a napkin. The coffee was almost ready, but not quite. He introduced himself. No, he was not a Franciscan. "Everyone thinks that," he mentioned. No, he was a *Jesuit*, a member of the Society of Jesus (SOJ). The Jesuits were known by and large as *educators*. But he didn't teach and he wasn't a priest. He was a "lay brother." Lay brothers served as cooks, buyers, treasurers and in many other skilled and unskilled positions, he explained, smiling kindly. Then he waited for Edna to speak.

She wasn't usually chatty but she told him about going into the convent and coming out of the convent. Now she was working part-time here at Blueberry Hill. And then the coffee was ready. First things first! Edna poured him a nice cup of coffee and then she had to wait on some other customers who'd just come in. Brother Flynn enjoyed his coffee and his puzzle. Then he was stumped and had finished his coffee. It was time to go.

"Maybe you can finish this puzzle," he said to Edna, getting his wallet out of his briefcase. It was a nice briefcase, and old brown leather one. He had a little trouble getting his wallet out of his briefcase. It was jam-packed with papers and file folders but he managed to retrieve a thin little wallet which contained a few thin bills. He fumbled around. The poor man of course had taken a vow of poverty.

"It would be my honor," Edna said, trying to snatch the bill out of his hand.

"No, that is not at all necessary," he said, speaking very quietly, snatching it back. "You see, the problem is that I only have a $100 bill. Can you take it?"

A hundred-dollar bill? She'd have to go ask the manager but it was ok. The manager had plenty of change in the back room.

"Oh, by the way, it's been lovely chatting with you—Edna is it?"

"Yes, Edna. Lovely chatting with you as well, Brother--."

"Flynn, Brother Flynn. Oh, and by the way. Where is my mind! You seem like such a pleasant person--and good at greeting the public. We're looking for a receptionist. I can see that you're happy here but this job is *full time with benefits*. It's the at JSTB, the Jesuit School of

Theology in Berkeley, just above Holy Hill. We need a front desk receptionist."

Full time with benefits, that was an attention-getter! He opened the Help Wanted section of the newspaper, circled the ad and handed it to her.

"Leaving a convent is a big change, I'm sure, but you might enjoy working for the Jesuits. You might enjoy being around people from a different religious community."

"I appreciate it. Thank you," Edna said.

"And if you're not in the market for a new job, maybe you'll enjoy the Jumble!" And with that, he left the newspaper on the counter and exited. You could hear the refrains of Fats Domino singing his top hit "Blueberry Hill" through the door.

After work, alone on the bus, she took out the Help Wanted section and looked at the listing again:

"Receptionist-Clerk/Typist, Admissions office. Jesuit School of Theology, Berkeley."

She considered her options. They were scarce, scarce as hen's teeth. She meditated and prayed on it into the wee hours of the night. By the next morning she'd decided just to stay where she was. She would just stay where she was at Blueberry Hill. And then, just as the morning rush was over and she was preparing a new urn of coffee, Brother Flynn came in again, limping a bit. He had something wrong with his leg but it didn't seem to bother him terribly. In fact, he seemed to be feeling quite cheerful.

"Guess what!" he exclaimed.

"I can't guess," Edna said, bringing him a napkin and a glass of water.

"I can't stay, thanks. But I told them about you at JSTB, about your leaving the convent and starting a new chapter in life. And they would like to meet you. They want you to come in and interview for the receptionist job! *Something* told me this just might work out. But I must dash."

He was on his way to a meeting. He handed her an envelope. Tucked inside was a job application form and a map of North Berkeley.

"Just fill this out and make an appointment for tomorrow, if you can. The phone number and address are at the top of the application, and I circled the location of the Administration Building on the map. What do you think?"

"God works in strange and mysterious ways!" Edna said, pleasantly shocked. Then she started to worry. "But office work. What about a typing test? I'm a bit rusty."

"I'll take care of it. All you have to do is fill out the form and call for an interview if you're interested. Are you interested?"

"Yes, I am interested!" Edna decided to take a chance. Why not? God does work in mysterious ways.

She filled out her application, made an appointment, and headed out the next morning for her interview. Fortunately, it was her day off at the bakery.

Chapter 10
"Holy Hill"

The Jesuit School of Theology at Berkeley (JSTB) was not technically on Holy Hill. It was actually a block or two higher up above the original *God Quad*. The original *Holy Hill* was just four protestant religious schools facing a plaza, designed to look like they'd been there for hundreds of years in old England or Europe. But the prettiest structures were built in the 1920's, designed by the Berkeley City Architect, Walter H. Ratcliff, Jr. Later the Jesuits moved in. Now Buddhists, Muslims and other religious institutions have moved into the Holy Hill neighborhood, but this was then.

Edna's convent was way above Holy Hill, high up in the Berkeley Hills on Grizzly Peak. From her convent windows Edna had often looked down on the slate rooftops and the spires below but most of the time all she saw were trees and fog. Holy Hill was on Northside, north of the U.C. campus and close to the Campanile. Getting off the bus, Edna could hear the bells ringing. It was just 9:00. She was early. Getting off at Le Conte and Euclid, the air just felt holy. It smelled holy, like jasmine, eucalyptus and pine trees. Birds sang. One could imagine St. Francis here, preaching to the sparrows. Edna headed up Euclid Avenue. The aroma of coffee filled the air. Cafes were abuzz. Buzz, buzz. The whole street was humming. Too much caffeine. Men in brown robes scurried past, Franciscan Friars, perhaps, or maybe Jesuit brothers? Who knew?

Around the corner on LeRoy Avenue she found a pale green stucco mansion guarded by two cement Chinese lions, the Administration Building. She walked up the stairs, passed the Chinese lions and made her way through the heavy carved wooden doors. It would be quiet when Edna arrived. She was still early. According to her instructions she was simply to enter, turn to her right and have a seat in The Lounge. Someone would come out to greet her at 9:30, or ASAP.

The Lounge was spectacular. It had high wood-beamed ceilings. Light poured in through the stained-glass windows and bounced off the shiny black lacquer surface of the grand piano, illuminating The Lounge with colorful rays. Tiny dust particles floated through the rainbows like fairy dust. Everything was silent. Long wooden benches with red velvet cushions lined one wall. The other walls were filled with books, floor to ceiling. Edna enjoyed a little free time to sit and pray and meditate. And then someone came out to get her.

Edna's interview with the Dean of Admissions went well. The Dean was a tall white man around 50, graying at the temples and wearing a nice beige suit. He looked like the kind of man who played golf, in lanky good shape. He was an administrator but he was also a priest, he explained. He just didn't wear his "blacks" every day. Their meeting was brief. He was just on his way out, he apologized. He had to catch a plane. He was going on vacation, to play golf! The Assistant Dean was already gone.

Edna gave him a very brief synopsis of her work experience in the convent and at Blueberry Hill Bakery. Very interesting. What they needed was someone to unlock the front door each morning, answer the phone, take messages, and greet visitors. She might be asked to do some typing. Could she type? Yes, she had taken Typing I and Typing II in high school but she was a little rusty. Fine. Everything seemed in order. The Dean promptly shook Edna's hand warmly and asked if she had any questions. No, everything seemed fine. The Dean did have one last question.

"I know this is pushing it but could you start right away?" He was just on his way out of town and was hoping to have this position filled ASAP.

"Yes," she could. "But I'd have to talk it over with my manager at the bakery."

"Yes, of course, that would only be right."

He thanked Edna for coming in and shook her hand warmly-- with TWO hands! Then he escorted her to the front door and vanished. Later that day the people at Blueberry Hill Bakery gave her a glowing recommendation and wished her the best of luck on her new job. "Don't let the door hit you in the ass," no one said. OK. Bye!

Edna was happy and the people at Blueberry Hill Bakery were happy, too. The people at the JSTB Administration Building were delighted.

They wouldn't have to hire a temp! The next day Edna had a job. She would start right away!

Chapter 11
"Sensible Shoes"

Edna had a new job, but wore her old shoes. She loved her old shoes. They were comfortable, black with thick black soles and thick black shoe laces, good walking shoes. Each morning Edna got dressed, put on her shoes, took the bus to work and walked up the stairs of the Administration Building and into the inner sanctum.

In the Lounge she opened the heavy maroon velvet drapes. Rays of light beamed through stained-glass windows. Dust particles floated through rainbows of light. After a moment of quiet meditation, she made her way into the Reception Area and turned on the overhead fluorescent lights. Then she opened the Venetian blinds and took a seat at the large wooden desk, called the answering service to retrieve messages and jotted them down on pink or sometimes yellow message pads.

With nothing left to do she practiced her typing. It was a slow week at JSTB, in-between semesters. At 10:00 the mail for the Dean and the Assistant Dean arrived. She opened it, sorted it, and took it to their desks. They were officially out on vacation.

One day she opened a letter from Sister Maria Giovanni (Lao, Chaoi-Mei) of the Sisters of the Precious Blood of Tokyo. She'd been accepted for a summer study program in Synoptic Gospels but belonged to an order of cloistered nuns who were *discalced*. They didn't wear shoes. Wearing shoes violated their vow of poverty; but not wearing shoes violated safety and sanitation standards elsewhere. She put that letter on top of the Assistant Dean's pile. Fingers crossed!

In Edna's convent nuns wore shoes. They were *calced*, not *discalced*. Her heart went out to Sister Maria Giovanni, she said to Brother Flynn. He'd stopped to chat. He was meeting someone in The Lounge. "Oh, don't worry, Edna. If she's got money to travel and a plane ticket, someone will find her some shoes."

Brother Flynn always wore brown leather shoes that had to be laced up. Other men in brown robes around Holy Hill often wore

41

sandals. Some of the sandals looked home-made. They were called "Tijuana treads". They were home-made with tire treads. Brother Flynn, as it turned out, happened to have a wooden leg and therefore a wooden foot, which required a special shoe. He couldn't wear sandals. His special shoes helped him walk better but he still had quite a LIMP. After a while you didn't notice it. You noticed his smile, a smile like Franklin Delano Roosevelt's in a limousine, waving at crowds.

"Temporal co-adjutor" was Brother Flynn's official title. Edna wasn't sure what that meant; she'd never studied Latin. But he was an adjunct, an added-on, a helper. That morning he was going to help a Franciscan. Franciscans were a *mendicant* order. They took their vows including the vow of poverty seriously.

"We do too; but not like THAT. Take this building for example," he continued, swirling an arm around in a grand circle. "The Jesuits bought it *cheap*. We bought it for a song. It used to be a fraternity house. Now there's a different kind of fraternity here. Hah!" In the future the Society of Jesus would buy more property, which would be used for more classrooms and more meeting halls. "If you want to have a school you need to have a *school house*, a *building*. We're just trying to be realistic."

This was where poor Franciscans came to borrow money, Brother Flynn mentioned to Edna, and then he greeted his poor guest and escorted him into the Lounge. At noon they emerged. He showed his friend to the door and made his way back to Edna at the reception desk. It was time for her lunch break, time for Brother Flynn to relieve her. This meant that she had to go to the cafeteria *alone*. She wished he could come along with her to the cafeteria but somebody had to sit at the front desk. Someone could walk in and ask a question.

The priests' cafeteria was right next door. It existed mainly to serve the teaching priests who lived in the residence hall above the cafeteria; but employees were welcome Monday through Friday. So far Edna seemed to be the only employee in the cafeteria that day; it was easy. All she had to do was select a hot entree, a sandwich, and/or a small salad. Sometimes there was soup. For desert there could be Jell-O, pudding, canned Mandarin orange sections, or sometimes ice-cream sandwiches.

After taking her tray and utensils, Edna selected some food and searched for a place to sit, eventually making her way to an empty table near a pleasant window where she could look at some bushes and think about God. And then she returned to her desk, still unhinged.

"What's wrong, Edna?" Brother Flynn asked.

"Nothing," she replied and went back to work.

Edna was not used to eating lunch with *men*. Around 2:30pm Edna pick up the mail for the Dean and the Assistant Dean in the basement. For some reason the mail wasn't delivered to her desk in the afternoon, but Edna LIKED going to the basement. It gave her a chance to peruse the notices on the Community Bulletin Board next to the mail boxes. The Bulletin Board was like a community newspaper. There were notices for "Employment Wanted/Offered" and areas for "Housing Wander/Offered."

Chapter 12
"No Poodle Skirts"

It was another slow week at JSTB. The Spring Semester was over; the Summer Session hadn't yet begun. There was ample time for Edna to learn her job and figure out what to wear to work. She couldn't wear her mother's pink wool suit forever. It was a lovely light-weight pale pink wool suit but it was getting too warm. Mrs. Reilly understood and wanted to help her daughter find some cute outfits. She searched her closet. It was a large closet packed with clothes. A few things fit Edna.

"Don't go to too much trouble, Mom."

"It is no trouble at all," Mrs. Reilly replied, looking through every item in her closet to see what Edna might look good in. "This would be fabulous on you!" She held up a baby blue silk suit with pleated skirt and matching jacket with a white silk scarf.

"This is silk," Edna pointed out. "I'm allergic to silk, Mom."

"Of course, of course,"

At least it was spring, too warm for fox furs and felt hats with feathers. Edna did find two comfortable old floral print cotton dresses, one size fits all.

"My old mu-mu's! These old things? You're crazy! I just wear them when I'm cleaning!" Mrs. Reilly explained, trying to grab them out of Edna's hands.

"But I love them, Mom. They'll be just fine! Nice and comfortable."

"Comfortable my eye, who cares!" She reached into her closet again and pulled out a skirt.

"What IS this, Mom?"

"It's a POODLE SKIRT, silly!"

It looked something like an old vinyl record or maybe a partially opened umbrella made of yellow felt with black felt poodles stitched on here and there. And what about a nice yellow sweater to match, or a black one? No, Mom. Thanks. And the pointed brassieres were surely not appropriate for the office, Mom!

"I can't Mom, I just can't. I'm not used to this," Edna said, as nicely as possible.

"Well, you can't very well wear my old mu-mu's every day, either. Can you? They'll think something is wrong with you. You were gone for a long time, Edna. You don't know what's in style now, sweetie, and you need a bra!"

Edna was outgunned. Her mother knew about fashion. And Edna would not get a paycheck for two more weeks and it was getting warmer. She couldn't wear that nice pink Channel suit forever. Edna and her mother went shopping. Just for basics. Some new underpants and a bra. Edna relented, gave in on that one. And some new socks.

"Your socks look like hell!" Edna's mother shrieked when she saw her daughter's old socks. "How many times have you darned them!"

"OK, OK, Mom," Edna said. "I darned them over and over."

Edna's mother was right. Edna's socks looked like hell. Her shoes weren't as bad; but they didn't go with the poodle skirt. Edna got a pair of plain black "flats." They were not as comfortable as her old shoes, but they didn't hurt, and she could walk to the bus stop in them.

"Nice skirt," the bus driver said. "I dig it."

"Thanks," Edna said. She didn't know if he was kidding or not.

It was nice and quiet at the Administration Building. It didn't matter much what Edna wore to work, at least not from the waist down. Her poodle skirt and shoes were hidden under her desk. Nobody was there anyway. Both the Dean of Admissions and the Assistant Dean of Admissions were off on vacation. Many professors were gone, too, on sabbatical or on retreat. Edna was basically alone that week, invisible. Sometimes the phone rang. "Hello, Jesuit School of Theology at Berkeley, How May I Help You?" Sometimes a priest or a lay person would walk through. "Good morning. Good morning".

Sometimes Brother Flynn might stop by for a minute. He was always busy as a bee but it was nice to see a friendly face now and then. Except for Brother Flynn, Edna didn't know a soul. Sometimes there was nothing to do but open the mail, and put it on piles for the Associate Dean and the Dean. Mail was still coming in from people who wanted to attend the Summer Session--too late! Summer classes were already filled, sorry! One applicant was Father Francis Xavier Collingwood of the White Fathers of Africa. He was originally from Rock Hill, Rock Chapel, County Cork, Ireland. But now he was stationed in Bolga Denga, Ghana and he was concerned about the water:

Catholic Parish, P.O. Box 15, Bolga Denga, U.R. Ghana
Dearest Friends at JSTB:
Greetings from Bolga Denga! I hope you are all well and happy, in God's hands. I am just writing this quick, follow-up note to inquire about the status of my application to study at JSTB this summer, or if not in the summer perhaps in the fall. I was hoping to have heard from you by now, but the mail here is not always reliable and we have no telephone...
With Very Best Wishes,
Your Friend in Christ,
Francis X. Collingwood, SJ

Edna put Father Callingwood's letter on the top of the Dean's pile of correspondence, so he'd be sure to find it upon his return. And then it was time for coffee break. At coffee break time Edna was allowed to scoot quickly over to the cafeteria and pick up something to bring back to her desk. One could get tea, coffee, juice, cereal, and fruit and anything else that happened to be left over from the priests' breakfast. Edna's favorites proved to be Tropical Punch and cinnamon rolls, but there was always *something*. And it was free! A perk of the job! And then there was lunch.

On Friday there were fish sticks, really good. Fresh, not frozen. If truth be told, Edna preferred lunch at the convent. She enjoyed silence. It was lovely. In the convent she had meals with other women, also dressed in black and white. Now she was the only woman in the cafeteria. Maybe she should wear something beige to go with the walls; but here she was in her yellow and black poodle skirt and matching yellow top. In the afternoons she went to the mail room and collected the afternoon mail, returned to her desk and sorted it. Then she practiced her typing.

Day after day that week, everything was the same. Edna arrived at the Administration Building, unlocked the doors, opened the drapes and blinds and turned on the lights. She listened to the phone messages and checked her in-box for typing. There was none. The morning mail arrived. She sorted it and then it was time for coffee break. She scooted over to the cafeteria for coffee and a cinnamon bun, and brought them back to her desk. At noon Brother Flynn came to relieve her for lunch. That day was an exceptionally quiet day.

"Where is everybody?" Brother Flynn asked.

"Good question," Edna replied.

"I have another question. I know you just left the convent. But is there some reason why you're wearing these strange outfits?"

"My mother loaned them to me," Edna replied. She wasn't much good at small talk. "I have two different skirts and two little sweaters. You can mix and match."

"I'll pretend like I didn't hear that, Edna. This isn't YOU. And I don't MEAN to be MEAN, but it looks like you cut your hair yourself."

"Yes."

He was no one to talk. He always had the same goofy haircut with the bald spot in the middle. Brother Flynn was no hairdo fashionista; but Edna was not the kind of example the Jesuit School of Theology wanted to present to the public. The Jesuits wanted to present an image of simplicity and functionality, the Assistant Dean proclaimed. No frills, no yellow poodle skirts with matching yellow bolero sweaters! "Get her some clothes!" the Assistant Dean repeated over the phone that morning to Brother Flynn. She was on vacation in Santa Cruz but her spies filled her in. "And can you get her a normal haircut?"

"Yes, I can."

"Or else!"

"OK, OK."

The following day at noon, instead of eating in the cafeteria, Brother Flynn and Edna grabbed some sandwiches to-go from the cafeteria and went shopping at the Goodwill of Berkeley. Edna returned with two comfortable white blouses and two plain navy-blue skirts. Edna liked them. Everyone would think she was still a nun. Now all she needed was an ordinary haircut, but her hair was still too short to cut. She'd just tried cutting it herself, again. Her hair would have to wait but at least Edna had a new uniform: white blouses and navy skirts.

"This one would look FABULOUS on you," Mrs. Reilly said, bringing one of her gently worn frocks over to her daughter at breakfast.

"Oh, thanks, Mom. What I'm wearing is good enough." Edna was already dressed in her Navy blue and white uniform.

"OK," Mrs. Reilly said, with a deep sigh. "If you don't meet a guy you can always go to college."

"Gotta go now. Bye, Mom!" Edna pretended she hadn't heard that last comment.

Then her mother relaxed again, lit a cigarette and enjoyed the peace and quiet of another eensy-weensy little cocktail.

Chapter 13
"Spiritual Exercises"

Edna did not miss the convent. Well, she did miss the convent
sometimes, but not enough to go back. Now there was no turning back.
Now she didn't even feel like going to church, she confessed to Brother
Flynn. She had no one else to confess to, and the convent had been her
church. She'd been LIVING IN A CHURCH. Dropping in for a few
hours now and then seemed pointless. Edna was facing a spiritual and
religious crisis. But Brother Flynn had an idea. He dashed into The
Lounge, pulled a book off a shelf and returned with a book. *The
Spiritual Exercises of Saint Ignatius.*

"You could try this!" he suggested. "It's like a self-guided
retreat. You could go on a real retreat but it would take four weeks. We
couldn't be without our receptionist for four weeks."

The *Spiritual Exercises* were designed for use in Catholic
retreats with a trained priest as a guide but a regular person could do
them alone, reading along with the book. The program was divided into
Four Weeks, or sections, but each section didn't have to be exactly a
week. They were just meant to be a rough outline, a *guide.* You could
go at your own pace, as long as you covered the basics:

> Week #1: meditate on your sins, on whatever separates you
> from God
> Week #2: meditate on Jesus' life
> Week #3: meditate on The Passion
> Week #4: meditate on the Resurrection and Ascension

Edna began Week #1 right away, with great relish and delight.
The purpose of Week #1 was to face one's sins, not just to wallow in
one's sins but to get to know them and let them go, and put one's life in
order and return to God.

Since leaving the convent Edna DID feel more separate from
God. Since moving in with her mother, Edna did feel lost. What was

she doing in her mother's house? What was she doing here at JSTB? Her mother's house and the reception desk at JSTB were both safe harbors in a storm of chaos but, she confessed to God, she really didn't know what she was doing or why she was reading this book by Saint Ignatius.

Instead of going on to Week #2, Edna became distracted and started looking through some of the other books in The Lounge. She'd already practiced her typing. She was up to speed. The Spring Semester was over and the Summer Session hadn't started yet. Sometimes Edna still had many hours with not much to do and so she began reading about *the life* of St. Ignatius, and the history of the Jesuits. The Reception Area was as silent as the convent often was. It was almost as if God wanted her to sit and read, and take notes.

She read and read, and stopped occasionally to think and to take notes. Maybe her mother was right. Maybe she SHOULD go to college. Here at JSTB she was already in college, working in a college and surrounded by books. But you never knew, she said to herself, "these notes might come in handy one day, maybe in a college classroom!" She could only agree with herself. Here are a few pages of Edna's notes, on the life of Saint Ignatius Loyola:

"The Life of St. Ignatius Loyola, notes by Edna Reilly"

The Society of Jesus ("The Jesuits") is a religious order of Roman Catholic Priests founded in the sixteenth century by Ignatius of Loyola (and his friend Francis Xavier). He was born in 1491 in the family castle in Castile in the Basque country; and inherited his family's sense of honor, duty and general superiority. He was educated in the grand style of the day and began his worldly career as an army officer and a carouser, always busy gambling, dueling, romancing, etc. At age 30, he led his soldiers into a hopeless battle against the French. He himself was seriously wounded in one leg and almost died.

During his long and painful convalescence, he began to study the lives of Jesus and the saints, particularly Saint Francis, and was inspired. He eventually recovered but with a serious limp, not unlike Brother Flynn's. After that, instead of going back into the army Ignatius set out on a pilgrimage to the Holy Land. He got as far as the caves in Manresa, not far from Barcelona but he was stopped by the Plague. Instead of traveling hopelessly onward on a fool's journey to death, he prayed, studied and sometimes self-flagellated, which was popular then in some religious circles. During this period of spiritual examination, Ignatius developed his famous "Spiritual Exercises." At age 33, in 1523 he began teaching his exercises at a Dominican priory.

Eventually he'd have to defend his Exercises against the Spanish Inquisition, but he soldiered on, fighting a "war against ignorance." The Inquisition arrested him and forbad him from speaking in public. But he did it again and was arrested again. A judge soon let him go. He just had to promise that he would not speak again on certain topics such as mortal versus venial sin.

At age 37 he pursued an advanced degree (and became roommates with Francis Xavier) at the University of Paris. In 1534 the two roommates and a few other friends started their own religious order, the "Society of Jesus." They took the traditional vows of poverty, chastity and obedience, and added another unwritten vow, the willingness to travel and readiness to teach, such as his colleague Jerome Nidal:

"Jerome Nidal early Jesuit, notes by Edna Reilly"
Jerome Nidal (1507-1580), an early and influential Jesuit, promoted the philosophy that "the world is our house," with or without geographical limits. Jesuits went all over the world, learning, and teaching. Sometimes they were treated as guests, and invited to dinner, sometimes treated as hostile invaders and killed. This was part of the Jesuits' larger "war on ignorance."

In 1540 Pope Paul III signed off and the Society of Jesus became official. Ignatius was elected the first Superior General of the Jesuits. He died in 1556, was declared a saint in 1622. His feast day is July 31. To this day St. Ignatius Loyola's "Spiritual Exercises" are used in many Catholic retreats for both *religious* and lay people.

Chapter 14
"The Inquisition"

For some reason, Edna returned to the Spiritual Exercises of Saint Ignatius of Loyola, and went on to Week #3, and meditated on Jesus' life and his *Passion.*

The word "passion" has its roots in the Latin word "patior" or "suffering." This reminds us of the saying, "passion is suffering." But in "the passion" in this case refers to Christ's suffering, which ended by death by crucifixion. After meditating on Jesus crucifixion Edna for no particular reason began studying the Spanish Inquisition. She read, and took notes:

"The Inquisition, notes by Edna Reilly"

The Inquisition was started to fight heresy. It was started by Pope Gregory IX and it began in France in 1184 but spread fast. By around 1250 most of the Inquisitors were in Rome. They were Dominicans, but some were Franciscans. The Inquisition spread to Spain and Portugal, and then to Cape Verde and Goa, next to Peru, Mexico, and Brazil, not necessarily in that order. Torture and executions multiplied. Punishments included:
-Fines
-Imprisonment
-Wearing a Red Letter sewn onto a garment (like the Scarlet Letter)
-Banishment
-Hanging
-Burning at the Stake
-Pouring water down your throat till your stomach almost explodes

In 1478 King Ferdinand II of Aragon and Queen Isabella of Castile began The Spanish Inquisition. It was originally supervised by people from the Dominican order, at a time before Jesuits existed. Some Jesuits were later involved later but not all. Some Jesuits resisted (see case of Galileo Galilei).

Punishments got worse and included:
-Hanging by your arms (in various positions) till your shoulders dislocated or your arms fell off

-Stretched on the rack till various joints dislocated or body parts or all of body separated
-Application of heated metal pincers
-Thumb screws
-Boots, that broke bones in your feet
-Burning body parts, especially feet
-Sitting on something sharp that goes up your butt with weights on your feet

The purpose was to get people to confess and repent. But there had been worse tortures before the Inquisition:
-Stuffing people into a barrel filled with shards of glass and/or knives
-Cutting off breasts or other body parts, including decapitation
-Crucifixion (classic from times past)
-Torture with hooks

St. Eulalia of Barcelona (290-303), for example, was decapitated, and a dove flew out of her neck. After St. Eulalia of Merida was burnt at the stake, around the same time, a dove flew out of her mouth.

       Edna was just getting started with her reading and note taking. It seemed like this free time would go on forever but soon enough all hell broke loose. Summer Session began! People started showed up, immediately! The Dean and the Assistant Dean of Admissions returned from their vacations. Teaching priests showed up. Students showed up, looking for places to live. Suddenly there was typing to do. Edna's in-box was packed to overflowing. And every time she saw Brother Flynn he was in a big rush. He'd give Edna a wave. Sometimes he winked. Instead of going on to work on "Week #4: Meditate on the Resurrection and Ascension" Edna had to start *working*. She'd have to meditate later because now a steady stream of people, mostly MEN, were walking in and out. In the cafeteria, it was shocking for Edna to be in a room with so many men. Once she saw another woman in the cafeteria wearing a nice floral print dress; but whoever she was she was busy talking and Edna never saw her again.
       Unlike nuns, of course, priests didn't wear *habits* or cover their heads with black and white contraptions. They walked around freely with naked heads, even bald heads sometimes. The main difference, of

course, was that priests wore pants and were allowed to perform the ritual of TRANSUBSTANTIATION, the ritual of turning communion wafers into the body and blood of Christ. Edna missed baking communion wafers. She wondered where these Jesuits purchased theirs. More would be revealed perhaps at a later date.

Chapter 15
"Summer Session"

The Summer Session was in full swing. People were buzzing about, looking for classrooms, buying books, upbeat. For many priests, coming to study at the Jesuit School of Theology at Berkeley was a plum assignment, especially in the summer. It wasn't too hot or too cold. And good news, Sister Maria Giovanni was granted permission to wear shoes and could come to Berkeley! Everyone at JSTB was happy for her. She could make the journey from Tokyo wearing shoes. Edna never saw Sister Maria Giovanni. She never saw Father Collins of the White Fathers of Bolga Denga' but he was needed in Ghana where he was.

The Summer Session began with a bang! Typing piled up. Visitors began stopping at the front desk, asking for directions and suggestions on where to find housing. Edna passed out free maps of Berkeley and pointed them in the direction of the Community Bulletin Board in the mail room for housing and part-time jobs if needed. Edna worked hard all morning and then it was time for lunch. The cafeteria was jam-packed with 40 or 50 professor-priests of all skin colors and tones. Most were wearing *blacks*, as opposed to brown robes or regular street clothes. Edna tried to blend in but it was impossible. For one thing, she was one of the few women in the cafeteria and the only person wearing a navy skirt and white blouse.

"This is how any minority feels," Edna said to herself as she walked into the cafeteria. There were men of all races here, mostly white men from all over the world, but no women. Well, there was one woman over near a window chatting with a group of priests. She was wearing a smart beige linen suit. Edna's instinct told her to avoid this woman. In the convent Edna had been part of a community. Here she was lost in a sea of strangers. Bravely she collected her tray, napkin, utensils and a tuna-egg salad sandwich with a side of coleslaw. Then she began hunting for an empty seat. It was crowded but she had to sit *somewhere*. There were no more empty *tables*. The best she could hope for was an empty *chair*. One priest noting her dilemma waved a friendly wave.

"Sister, over here! We have an empty seat over here!"
Edna was pleased. Someone thought she was a nun, and called her *Sister*. She made her way through the human jungle to the empty chair. Her procession to this chair was long and arduous but she managed to sit down, nerves jangled.

"Thank you," she smiled to the kindly priest who had invited her over.

"We are pleased that you joined us," he smiled back.

Edna unloaded her food items from her tray, put the tray onto a stack of other trays nearby and faced the music. Now there was nothing to do but sit down, say hello and eat her lunch.

In the cafeteria, one could meet many new people. One had no choice. Jesuits were *supposed* to sit with new people at lunch every day, as a way to build community and avoid the development of social cliques. So here she was, Edna Reilly, sitting with a group of priests, not exactly part of the community but adjunct to the community; and if she wanted to have a free and convenient lunch, this was the best place. She could have gone around the corner and paid for her lunch somewhere on Euclid Avenue and come back to her desk five minutes late. But this was the only place where she could eat for free and be back at her desk in time for Brother Flynn to have his lunch before the cafeteria closed.

The friendly one at this table happened to be Father Mike from Milwaukee. The other priests at the table all seemed to look down at their plates, silently. In the convent Edna had been used to eating lunch this way, too, not looking at anyone or speaking. Here in the JSTB cafeteria, however, you were supposed to look up at people and talk to them. Fortunately, Father Mike was in his element and was happily munching away on a carrot stick.

"Call me Mike," he smiled at Edna, breaking the ice.

"Edna," Edna said. It took everything she had but she did it; she spoke. "I'm Edna."

It wasn't easy for Edna to sit here with all strangers, all men. *Mike* was sitting next to one priest who relentlessly looked down at his

56

grilled cheese sandwich but with a little coaxing from Mike, he was only too happy to share with the group. While he spoke, Edna began to enjoy her tuna-egg sandwich and coleslaw and feel better. Maybe it was just low blood sugar. In any event, this shy new person had just come from Washington, D.C. where he worked at a shelter for battered women, victims of domestic violence. It was discouraging work, he said, because you could spend days and days counseling a woman who was getting beaten up, getting abused. The woman would seek shelter and stay for a while and then go right back home to her abuser. Usually the victim was a woman and the abuser a man; but there were Lesbian abusers, too. And men were victims, too, but not usually. Sometimes prostitutes came to stay just for a rest, but went right back out on the street again after they got rested up. It was discouraging work. He took an angry bite of his grilled cheese. "It's a big relief to be here, I'm telling you," he added and took another nice big bite. There was a lull in the conversation.

Father Mike of Milwaukee changed the subject. He said that he worked in the prison system in Milwaukee and found a lot of different ways to help people out, he said, changing the subject, inviting others to join in. Edna had never been in a prison before, she managed to say, trying to be part of things. Another silence. Nobody else at the table had been in a prison either, not as a prisoner nor as a worker. People tried to talk about the weather. It was very pleasant, not too hot and not too cold.

Chapter 16
"TGIF!"

And then it was Friday. At lunch time Edna collected her tray, utensils and napkin, and Fish Sticks. It was Friday, traditionally fish day for Catholics. Edna had fish for lunch with everyone else. The afternoon went by and then it was 5:00. Time for Happy Hour. TGIF! Brother Flynn had been busy organizing a cocktail hour in The Lounge for priests and their guests--even a few women. Edna tidied up her desk, hoping that Brother Flynn would invite her to stay and join the fun as his guest but no. He continued to buzz around. Bzz, bzz. Now it was time for her to go away. Edna was neither a Jesuit nor a guest. She was an employee. OK. Bye. See you Monday. She wanted to stay and be *happy* with the others but off she went to the bus stop to go home and be *happy* with her mother.

Mrs. Reilly was waiting with a pitcher of Margaritas. She'd already put a good dent in it. "TGIF!" she said, getting up from her kitchen chair to give Edna a big hug. Then she poured Edna a nice Margarita and proposed a toast. "To Bigger and Better Things! Bottom's UP!" Edna took a little sip, and then just sat and stirred hers with a plastic straw. Her mother felt sorry for her. Poor Edna.

"It's hard being single when you're older," her mother commiserated. She knew how that felt. "Try the bar at the Sheraton downtown," she suggested.

But there was no bar at the Sheraton in downtown. There was no Sheraton in downtown El Cerrito. There was almost no downtown in El Cerrito. Edna was meeting men every day. They just weren't *available*. They were *priests*. Edna wasn't even a nun anymore; she was just a person, almost *nothing*.

"Maybe you should just move on," Mrs. Reilly said. "You're still young. Don't you WANT to get married?"

"I don't know..." Edna managed. Her only husband so far had been Jesus, and that was over. She changed the subject.

"What about you, Mom? Don't you want to get married again?"

"Well," Mrs. Reilly managed. "I already found someone."

"You did?" Edna asked, surprised. "Is it that man who calls you every night from Arizona?"

"Yes, that's him, that's my Prince Charming!"

"Do you want to marry him, Mom?"

"Yes."

"Why don't you?"

"He's already married, still married!"

"Oh."

"That's why he's down in Lake Havisu City, till the divorce is finalized. And he's looking into business opportunities."

"Oh."

At 7:30 as usual the phone rang. It was Prince Charming. Edna's mother went into her *boudoir* to answer the call on her pink Princess Phone. She was gone for quite a while.

On Sunday morning Edna considered joining a church, making friends with people after mass. But after being in the convent she just didn't feel like it for some reason. The weekend came and went. And then it was Sunday evening, time for the next exciting episode of *Gunsmoke*, with James Arness as Matt Dillon. It was Edna's favorite program and her favorite time of the week and her favorite program. She loved "Gunsmoke." She loved Miss Kitty and Marshall Dillon and Chester and Doc. She began to feel that they were a part of her life, part of her family. She wished she could watch "Gunsmoke" every night.

Edna made the best of it. She hopped into bed on Sunday night and was just getting comfy under the covers when she heard a voice. She sat up straight in bed and listened more closely. There was no doubt. It was the Voice of God but it sounded different, very different.

"Hello, Edna?" The Voice of God spoke in a different voice, in a contralto, or maybe an alto, the voice of a woman.

"Yes!" Edna replied, delighted. "Is it you, God? You sound different."

"I am different. I change! I am now a contralto, or maybe an alto. I'm Dinah Shore.

"Dinah Shore!"

"Yes, Edna. And how have you been since leaving the convent?"

59

"Well..." Edna found it hard to speak, in front of Dinah Shore.

"Edna, tell me something" the Voice of God as Dinah Shore said, "tell me, have you found anything to enjoy recently? That's my specialty. Feel good, try to!"

"I can't, ah..."

"Just spit it out. I know you that *Gunsmoke* is something you enjoy very much, do you not?" the Voice of God as Dinah Shore said.

"Yes, I'm ashamed to say."

"Ashamed, why ashamed, sweetheart?"

"Well, it's nobody's spiritual calling, is it?"

"Oh, come on now. What I'm getting at here is, would you go so far as to say you've found at least a little bitty bit of bliss watching *Gunsmoke* at all?

"Well, kind of." It was hard for Edna to admit that something so minor and frivolous could bring joy. "It's so trivial, isn't it?"

"Trivial? No, not at all. Why, I'd say that *Gunsmoke* is a moral tale; each episode dramatizes a choice between right and wrong, good and evil. How could that be trivial? I encourage you to take a wider view and ease up a little, sweetie. Take me. I got polio when I was a toddler. My parents helped me for years to get over it, but I still have a little limp now and then.

"You had polio?"

"Yes, there's still something wrong with one of my feet. But I still let my soul enjoy living. I see the USA in my Chevrolet. Sometimes I still limp a little, but they don't show this on TV, no, not on the Dinah Shore Show!"

In 1958 TV was still in its infancy, at least in its youth. Edna was rapidly advancing into middle-age. It was a shame since she hadn't finished being young in the first place.

Chapter 17
"Bliss"

On Monday morning Edna had a lot of typing in her in-box. She typed and typed. Professors were starting to prepare for the Fall Semester. At the end of the week much of Edna's work remained undone. She began to pray that God would get her out of the office one day. Her only consolation was TV. And *Gunsmoke*.

"Hello, Edna!" the Voice of God spaketh in the voice of the noted Italian tenor Mario del Monico. God waited till the latest episode was over and her mother was passed out on the couch. "How's is going? Como esta? Buona sera!"

"Well, fine, bueno. And by the way you sound Spanish, or Italian?"

"Yes, either/or. I am all things to all people, visible and invisible. I'm having some trouble mastering Chinese but this is a conversation for another time. I sense a dissatisfaction, a sadness, my child. What is the problem, per favore?"

"Well, my problem is my job. Even though it's full-time with benefits I'm thinking I was better off back in the convent."

"Mi dispiace. Excuse me, Edna," the Voice of God as Mario del Monaco interrupted. "I was hoping you'd come up with a better idea, something better than going back where you came from, something more *blissful*."

"Well," Edna mumbled, "there is one small thought that gives me hope for the future."

"Si si! We Italian and Spaniards are passionate. We are not patient. Say it! Speak to me!"

"Very well," Edna replied calmly and quietly. "I love watching *Gunsmoke* on TV. I love the drama, the characterization, the acting, the writing."

"That's IT? Nothing more? All you want to do is sit and watch *Gunsmoke*? Tell me your dream, darling! Think OPERA."

"Very well. OK. Um, I don't just want to sit and watch it. What I'd really like to do is go to Hollywood and write an episode for *Gunsmoke*."

"That's IT, bella, using your talents for one hour of bliss?"

"Well, um, yes."

"Forgive me, my dear, but I am on my way to the Teatro all Scala. La Scala to you. I, Mario del Monaco will give my 241st performance of Otello. You, on the other hand, with all your talent will stop at ONE episode of your most cherished *programma*?"

"Well, maybe after I wrote one or two episodes for *Gunsmoke*, I might try writing a whole script for a movie."

"Molto bene! And?"

"And then I'd write an award-winning screen play, a block-buster and win an Oscar!"

"Grazie, bella!"

"Then I'd buy a bungalow in Hawaii, with a veranda and a nice view. But really and truly I'd be delighted just to write one single episode for 'Gunsmoke.' I have some great ideas for Miss Kitty and Matt Dillon and Chester, a romantic triangle. Edna had lots more to say on this topic. She'd been contemplating various episodes of this program for weeks now. Yes, she'd been thinking about it, she continued to explain to God, but she was afraid to mention it in her prayers. And bungalow in Hawaii! There was a slight snoring noise.

"God, is that you? Are you sleeping!"

"No, no, no," the Voice of God as Mario del Monaco lied, "just resting my eyes. I have a big performance tonight. But getting back to you. My child, I am familiar with the entertainment business. Over ten million people have this same idea all over the USA and beyond, to go to Hollywood and write for TV. It can be done but there is much competition. I must be honest. If this is your heart's desire, I can fix it for you to write an episode of 'Gunsmoke,' but before I do that you must complete three great tasks. Will you go to any length, overcome all obstacles?"

"Yes!"

"Very well. Obey me and receive your reward! Your three great tasks are to write three books, get them published with good reviews in the *New York Times*, and come back with a track record."

"Three books? Good reviews in a major newspaper?"

"Not *a major newspaper*--the *New York Times*. Have a problem with that?"

"No, but what will I write ABOUT?"

"Me, I'm Italian. Opera is in my blood. You, however, are American. TV is in your blood. It should be easy. All of America is on the second-grade level. Don't make it too complicated, stick to popular themes, and don't make it too long."

And with that, the Voice of God as Mario del Monaco faded away.

Chapter 18
"Brainstorm"

Edna got out a piece of paper and a pencil, started thinking and came up with ideas for three books. The first was the most obvious:

Idea #1, "The Story of One Nun"

A cloistered convent somewhere in California. One woman's personal experiences. It was Edna's own story but would fictionalize it: change her name, change her hair, give herself a talent for math and science and introduce a love element, maybe a handsome doctor out in the jungles of far-off Africa. In the end she decided that "The Story of One Nun" wouldn't likely be a best-seller or a blockbuster in Hollywood either. Who would want to hear about life in a convent or in a hospital out in the jungle? Who'd believe it?

Note:
A movie entitled "The Nun's Story" would be a blockbuster smash-hit, later *that* year starring Audrey Hepburn. It came out in theaters everywhere and became a beloved film classic. Too bad Edna didn't drop out of the convent and write this story earlier. By 1958 the filming had already have been completed. Edna had a good idea, too little too late!

Idea #2, "Limericks"

Limerick, Ireland. A woman is stuck with a husband who drinks up all of his paycheck in a bar week after week, a landlord who will not fix the leaky roof, and a child who was desperately sick with pneumonia during the Potato Famine. Edna thought she might start each chapter or episode with a *limerick*, a bit of *Irish humor*, which she thought everyone would love. In the end, Edna decided that nobody would like it and nobody would believe it. Who would believe that the British would actually let people starve to death while the fish they so desperately needed and caught off their own shores were sold elsewhere for the sake of profit? Who would believe that a man would actually take all the money needed by his sick child and spend it at the bar? Everyone knows of landlords who don't fix the leaky roof, of course but that was the least of it.

Note: Many years later, a book entitled "Angela's Ashes" won hearts and minds, and was a best-seller and a blockbuster smash hit, but not for many years. Edna was too far ahead of her time.

Idea #3: The Life of Jerome Nidal and the Jesuits (1507-1580):

An early and influential Jesuit, he promoted the philosophy that "the world is our house," a world with or without geographical limits. As Jesuits went all over the world, learning and teaching, they were sometimes treated as guests and invited to dinner, and sometimes treated as hostile invaders and killed. This was part of the Jesuits' larger "war on ignorance." This story had a lot of violence in it. Edna thought this just might be a best-seller and a Hollywood blockbuster.

Note: Off in the future a famous Hollywood actor Robert DeNiro would star in a violent historic movie about Jesuits abroad. It was not a success. Maybe if she'd tried, Edna could have written a better screenplay and got to meet Robert DeNiro. Too bad.

Edna crumpled up another piece of paper. She was at work, at her desk at JSTB. Things had slowed down a bit. Edna had a break in the action, and took a little time to think about her writing projects. Nothing seemed right. Just then Brother Flynn showed up to relieve her so she could go to the cafeteria.

"Time for lunch!" he said happily and then noticed the sad look on her face. "Edna, what's wrong?"

"I was just trying to come up with an idea for a book," she confessed, and then just spit it out. "I'm trying to come up with an idea for a book which could become a best-seller and be optioned in Hollywood and lead to a block-buster movie." She waited for Brother Flynn to start laughing but he didn't.

"Great idea, fantastic!" he said. "You have a perfect story standing right in front of you. Just take a look."

"Alright," Edna said, and looked around. "You mean write about JSTB?"

"No. Right in front of you. You can write about me! My life has Hollywood written all over it. Let's be honest. I'm a good-looking older guy in a brown robe, with a wooden leg. I have a STORY."

Edna sat quietly. That could be true but she'd never written a book before and didn't know how, she continued with her confession. But Brother Flynn had complete confidence and was ready to start immediately. "Are you kidding me? This story could be GREAT!" he exclaimed over and over. "You can do it. I know you can." He slept on it and began to have second thoughts. He changed his mind. It just wouldn't DO to have his whole life story told to *the world.* Edna was disappointed but Brother Flynn had another idea.

"I know a wonderful guy. He's not a priest anymore. He's a *former* priest. He's got a terrific story. He'll be happy to tell you the whole thing; you might just have your best-seller right there. And he's an EX-priest--he has nothing to lose by telling the whole thing."

Neither did Edna. She thought about Brother Flynn's idea. Maybe there *was* more than enough drama in the everyday life of a good, decent pries. Maybe even more-so in the life of an *ex-priest.* The drama of examining one's conscience was far from boring. And he'd left his vocation, as she had. Although he was a man, maybe she could relate to his story on some level.

"OK," she said to Brother Flynn, after returning from lunch. "I'd like to give it a try. I'd like to talk to your friend."

"That's great news! I already called Tom while you were in the cafeteria. He'd be happy to talk with you. You could interview him this weekend. Just go ahead, see what happens, and take it from there."

"OK," Edna agreed. "OK!"

Edna didn't know how to interview anyone. She didn't even have a tape recorder but she was a good note taker. Former Father Tom agreed to meet her the following Saturday at the Euclid Café. It was her first interview, the first of many, she hoped. Who could know? The result of that interview looked something like this:

"Interview #1, with Former-Father Tom"
(as told to Edna Reilly)

"It all started with Dorothy Day. She started the Catholic Worker Movement in the 30's, and set up soup kitchens in the Bowery. She was always trying to stir something up. Get it? Stir something up! Hah! You probably never heard of her. I'm from an older generation but to me she was the opposite of the Nazis, the opposite of people like Fritz Kuhn and Father Coughlin.

I was there in New York in 1939. There was a big Nazi rally at Madison Square Garden. Fritz Kuhn, called the "American Hitler," spoke. It was a huge rally. I started thinking about the priesthood then. As a Catholic, Father Coughlin bothered me the most. Father Coughlin used to get on the radio and stir up hatred of Jews, and spoke in favor of Hitler, Mussolini and Hirohito. He encouraged gangs of Fascists to go up against Jews and people in the labor movement.

Anyway, Dorothy Day converted to Catholicism. I don't know why. The Salvation Army had soup kitchens, too; but you had to listen to their spiel before you got to eat. Not at Dorothy Day's soup kitchens. You just ate, period. She believed in "distributism" and this was a third way, an alternative to capitalism or communism, a way to provide the basics for everyone without resorting to violence. Anyway, I was very bookish. That's how I heard about Dorothy Day, from the periodical "The Catholic Worker."

For a while I was a Franciscan because he cared about all God's creatures, the birds, the poor, all creatures. Everyone loved St. Francis. Now even lay people want to be Franciscans, so you have the Third Order of Lay Franciscans. And St. Francis didn't even believe in theology. He thought it was a waste of time! But I originally entered the priesthood because of Dorothy Day and her service to the poor. At some point, I concluded that Dorothy Day's IDEAS were just as important as her SOUP KITCHENS.

Later I switched over to the Jesuits. For years all I did was read. The Jesuits totally encourage and supported me in this. Eventually I earned several advanced degrees. For a long time, I felt a certain satisfaction in teaching, in sharing with my students. The Jesuits, this is their reason for being. But I started to feel that I'd lost touch with the reason why I originally went into the priesthood, because of Dorothy Day.

At some point I read "Authority in the Church," a Jesuit writing by John L. McKenzie. It explains the whole thing about religion and authority. After that I left the Jesuits, too. I left because I just wasn't following in the footsteps of Dorothy Day any more, and that's what it was really about.

I left the priesthood. Sleep out in the streets in neighborhoods where seven out of ten kids spend half their lives or more. The basic thing about being a priest-- one of them--is the vow of poverty. But you take the vow of poverty not to deliberately be poor, but so you can share and identify with the poor. What good are you if you don't even understand what it's like. But if you're poor, too... The basic thing is to live with people. Burn down the cloisters! Live with people! Live with the dying. Dying people are still alive, too! It's part of life."

"And that's it, Edna, in a nutshell," Tom said, wrapping it up. "One problem I still have is that I dropped out at age 65. I have no retirement or pension benefits--nothing. Now I have two part-time jobs. Whatever I can find. The problem is that two part-time jobs don't equal one full-time job. I have no health insurance, but many millions of people don't either. The best thing to do is go for a walk every day, don't smoke, and stay off motorcycles."

Edna thanked him for his time and headed for the bus stop. By the time she got home she doubted that this story would ever be a best-seller. For one thing, it was too short.

Chapter 19
"Mother Gets Married"

Mrs. Reilly put the receiver of her pink Princess Phone back on its pink cradle. HAPPY NEWS! She opened her bedroom door, and stepped out into the hallway.

Edna was busy watching "Gunsmoke." At least there's ONE normal thing Edna does, Mrs. Reilly thought. She knew that Edna was in the middle of her favorite show but she couldn't wait to share the news with Edna, BIG news! Well, maybe a nice drinky-poo first. Mrs. Reilly poured herself a high-octane sized vodka with an ice cube, and added one olive. And presto change-o, an instant martini! And THEN she went into the living room and scooted in next to her daughter on the couch. Edna was deeply involved in an episode of "Gunsmoke," which was almost over. Fortunately, it was time for a commercial but for once Mrs. Reilly didn't care what was on TV. She had something to say.

"I have something important to tell you," Mrs. Reilly said, afraid to say it. She even put her martini down.

"OK, Mom," Edna said, turning off the TV.

"You don't have to turn off the TV!" Mrs. Reilly insisted.

"OK," Edna said, happily turning the TV back on. "Mom, is something wrong?" Edna took her mother's hand. "What is it?" Edna looked at her mother and prepared for whatever news her mother had to deliver.

"Oh, I forgot something. I'll be right back. Watch the end of your show. It's almost over. I'll tell you after."

Mrs. Reilly was dying to tell Edna her news; but first she wanted to go out and have a cigarette, and Edna wanted to watch the end of her show. A few minutes later "Gunsmoke" was over. Mrs. Reilly had smoked her cigarette and returned to her daughter's side.

"OK!" Mrs. Reilly managed.

"OK!" Edna chimed in.

"Well," Mrs. Reilly managed, taking another sip of her martini, setting it back down. "Well, I just spoke to Mr. Blumenthal."

Edna had a bad feeling about this. She dreaded it but finally her mother took a deep breath and spit it out. "Mr. Blumenthal got a divorce!" Mrs. Reilly was thrilled. Edna just sat there. And *then* it started to sink in. Mr. Blumenthal was a real person. His divorce was just *finalized*.

"I see," Edna said, trying to look cheerful. Does that mean you'll be getting married now?"

"Yes!" her mother sang out, put her martini down, and gave her daughter a big hug, a great big hug. "Yes!"

Now that Mr. Blumenthal was now legally divorced, he and her mother could get *married*.

Her mother started packing her suitcases and a steamer trunk immediately. But she kept thinking of more things she needed. Mrs. Reilly was finally ready to go. She was *eloping*.

"I'm all ready to go!" Mrs. Reilly said, "to Lake Havisu City! I'm going to get married, to my snookie snookums!"

Edna's mother was actually was going to Arizona, to get married! She was driving to Arizona, alone, but she could do it. No problem. Soon she would be *Mrs. Blumenthal*. That morning Mrs. Reilly put on her new straw hat, the one with built-in sunglasses, had a few shots of vodka and refreshed her lipstick. Then she slipped in behind the driver's seat of her car and pressed her foot down on the gas pedal and away she went. See the USA in your Chevrolet! In Edna's opinion, her mother was going way too FAST, not driving too fast necessarily, but too fast for someone who just had a few shots of vodka. But there was no stopping Mrs. Reilly now. Edna had no influence, none at all. Just as her mother had had no influence over her. But the next step would be WORSE for Edna. Edna's mother was going to SELL THE HOUSE!

"I'll have to sell the house," Edna's mother explained over the phone a few weeks later. "Your father's life insurance wasn't going to last FOREVER! And Sidney's alimony and child support are going to cost him a PRETTY PENNY. "But he is my peach! He's my peachy-pie!"

"Mom, I just want you to be happy," Edna said honestly, kind of honestly.

70

Days later Mrs. Reilly, Edna's mother, became Mrs. Blumenthal. It was hard for Edna to believe. Sidney Blumenthal's first wife kept the name "Mrs. Blumenthal," and so there were two of them. But Edna's mother tried not to think about HER. Edna's mother had lived the life of a lonely widow for a long time. The brightest spots in her days were trips to El Cerrito Wine and Spirits, to see Mr. Blumenthal. Not that he was in any way responsible for Edna's mother's alcoholism. Before she got to know Sidney, Mrs. Reilly had been enjoying her cocktails very regularly, which started to become more evident as she slowly began to sober up. Mr. Blumenthal was delighted.

"You don't need that garbage anymore. We have each other, snookums!" he said, every day until she quit.

"Yes, we do have each other, poopsie," Mrs. Blumenthal agreed. "Alcohol, it's just empty calories! But what about that motel? Are we buying the motel or what?"

Edna's mother had no choice but to sell the family home, she explained to Edna over the phone. "We need the money! And this could benefit you, too. And besides, you never liked the house."

True. Edna's fondest dream had once been to get OUT of that house. Now, facing the loss of the family home, she felt sad and afraid. She got up the next day and took the bus to work.

Chapter 20
"First Decent Offer"

Edna's mother put the house on the market and would accept the first decent offer. "You can always join us in Lake Havisu City. We're going to buy The Lake Havisu Motel as soon as the house sells! We'll have plenty of rooms and plenty of work! It'll be grand!"

It would not be grand for Edna, living AND working at the motel. Her mother was no longer Mrs. Reilly but *Mrs. Blumenthal.* Edna was the only REILLY left in her family. Well, she had some aunts and uncles and cousins in New Jersey but they were on her *father's side* of the family. Her mother never cared much for them. Edna even considered going to New Jersey to meet them but couldn't afford it, especially not *now.* Soon the house would have to be emptied out. Most of the money from the sale of the house would have to be invested in *the motel.* Edna understood that she could move to Arizona, at least. She'd always have a job and a place to live waiting for her, at least.

"You know that, right? Sidney and I would love to have you come down and join us, Edna" her mother said, completely sober. "We're going to be working hard in the motel and you're always welcome. When the house sells, I'll be setting aside a little money for you but it won't be a LOT after the deductions, and then for the *motel.* It's all I can do for you. Otherwise you're on your own, kiddo. And by the way, I'm in AA!"

Edna was always shocked when her mother called, sober. She was used to her the other way but now her mother was in AA, and sober. It was hard to believe, but true. This move had been a good thing for her. Getting married again was a good thing. Now *the Blumenthals* enjoyed going out for milkshakes for fun. *Mr. and Mrs. Blumenthal* even quit smoking!

"Who needs that junk!" he said.

"I threw away my last two packs yesterday," she said. "Sidney said he'd divorce me if I didn't! Hah!"

72

And so Mrs. Reilly became Mrs. Blumenthal. She'd never been religious and never went to church, even when she was living with her late first husband who was a Catholic. Now that she was married to a Jew, for once in her life she had a spiritual practice, AA. But aside from that she and her husband were both *secular*. He didn't go to a synagogue and she didn't go to a church. Edna's mother had a new life, in any event. Now Edna was going to have to get one. But new lives take time.

The Blumenthals' bid on the motel, for example, was contingent on the sale of *Eleanora's* house, the Reilly family home. While they waited *The Blumenthals* rented a nice Air Stream Trailer. It was hooked up to utilities and was nestled into a cute little trailer park with lots of pretty palm trees--and an outdoor grill! Yes, Edna's mother had already begun a new life, but where did that leave Edna? Unprepared. One day she'd have to move out.

The phone rang. It was Edna's mother. She called every night from Lake Havisu City at 7:30 just to chat but this time she had *news*. "A real estate agent will be in to show the house around so just go shopping or something while she's making her sales pitch, OK, sweetie?" The words rang in Edna's ears like a bad case of tinnitus.

On Saturday morning the real estate agent was on her way over with a client! Edna managed to get up and get out before they arrived. Her instinct told her to go to JSTB. The Administration Building would be closed of course but Edna had a key. She opened the heavy carved wooden doors, and made a bee-line down to the mail room to see if there were any new listings on the "Housing Offered" section of Community Bulletin Board. And whom did she bump into but Brother Flynn!

"Edna, we don't usually see you on Saturday."

"No."

"You don't look well. What is wrong?"

"Nothing."

"What TYPE of nothing."

"My mother got married. She's selling the house. I have to move out. I need to find a room to rent."

"Wonderful! You know, Edna, I used to be a tax attorney. I've done taxes for lots of people around here. I might have an idea for you."

Chapter 21
"The Fixer"

Within the Society of Jesus (SOJ) Brother Flynn was known by the
jovial term "The Fixer." If you needed anything fixed, he took care of it-
-a spare tire or a real estate deal. In his previous incarnation he was a
tax attorney. He entered the SOJ as a "brother" or "coadjutor" and
served the community as a whole. Brother Flynn was "The Fixer."

"They call me 'The Fixer' around here, Edna. If you need
ANYTHING, just ask. I'll try to help you."

"Thanks."

On Monday Morning Edna went into work as usual, and
watched light rays beaming through the stained glass. Then she
checked for messages with the answering service. Then she sat and
stared into space. It did not go un-noticed. Brother Flynn had done
everything he could to help her adapt to her new job, to FIX IT; but it
didn't seem to be working out, not from the point of view of The
Assistant Dean.

"Why is this unfortunate woman sitting at the front desk,
GREETING people, may I ask?" she asked Brother Flynn. "How did she
even get in here? All she does is read and stare into space."

"I thought it would work out in time," he replied.

"Well, we're running out of time. The Fall Semester will be
here before you know it and she is not a good fit. You need to fix this.
Or we will!"

"OK, OK, I'll fix it!" he replied with a heavy sigh.

The week went by. At long last Friday. Thank God It Was
Friday, and Edna was especially thankful that the family home hadn't
sold! That real estate deal fell through, giving Edna a reprieve. She
wasn't ready to look for a new place to live. She didn't have the
strength. All she could do was lie down.

Depression makes people feel tired and listless. Edna spent
much of Saturday in prayer, staring into space, and lying down
watching TV. On Sunday she did the same thing. Happily, no more real

estate agents called. On Sunday evening she turned the TV on to her favorite show, *Gunsmoke*. During a commercial break Edna gathered all her strength and went into the kitchen to get a snack. She was hungry. She didn't have much in the refrigerator. She hadn't had the energy to do any grocery shopping that week. But there was a bag of potato chips in the cupboard.

She was busy opening the potato chips when she heard a voice. At first, she thought it was the Voice of God but it didn't sound familiar. Figuring that it was just a voice from the TV set, she put a few chips in a small bowl and headed back to the couch to watch the rest of her show when the Voice came back, louder.

"Shalom, Edna! Shalom! Do I have to get you a hearing aid? How many times do I have to say *Shalom*?"

"God, is it you?"

"Yes. Expecting someone else?"

"No, but you sound different, like a woman."

"Have a problem with women? Of course, I'm a woman. I'm Dinah Shore. It's just that I'm Jewish and I've never learned any Yiddish. I'm practicing to be a Jewish mother. I have two kids, you know."

"You're Jewish?"

"Yes. People used to wonder. There was a rumor going around that I was black. They knew there was something funny about me, but I am Jewish. I am all things but today I'm a Jewish mother. Everyone needs a Jewish mother now and then. So, Edna. I have a treat for you, *bubelah*, and it's no little *tchatchke*. But enough *mishegas*. I have a request. Actually, it's a commandment, one single commandment—not TEN commandments, just ONE. Is that too much to ask?"

"No. Absolutely not, God--Goddess!"

"Let's just stick with GOD. It carries more weight. Zeus is a god; Juno is a goddess; she just holds the coats while he cavorts. Know what I mean? OK. Listen carefully. I know you want to get back to your TV show, but this will only take a minute. Are you listening?"

"Yes, God. I'm all ears."

"Good. Since I am God, I command you to go to bed early, wake up well rested in the morning, and whatever comes your way just say

YES. Can you do that for me, bubelah? Can you just say YES no matter what just for 24 little hours?"

"YES," Edna managed. She was still feeling tired and listless. She just wanted to watch the rest of "Gunsmoke" and eat a few potato chips; but she listened patiently as God repeated the commandment and finally went away.

As God commanded Edna got up on Monday morning well rested and went to work. By mid-morning she was starting to feel depressed again. Even coffee didn't help. All morning she practiced saying YES but nothing unusual happened. People seemed to be avoiding her for some reason, and so she had plenty of time to sit quietly and stare into space or read, occasionally answering the phone. She could barely stay awake. Depression sometimes makes people feel tired and listless.

At lunch time Brother Flynn showed up to relieve her as usual, mayb just a few minutes late. And he was in a bit of a rush, brown robe all aflutter, looking very happy.

"I have news for you Edna. A housing possibility--a brand new situation!" he beamed. "Are you interested?"

"YES," Edna forced herself to say, almost falling asleep at her desk.

He took a piece of paper out of a secret pocket inside his brown robes somewhere and handed it to her.

"This is the address of a dear friend of mine, an old client. I still do her taxes. She lives just a couple of blocks away, around the corner off LeConte. She's a real sweetheart and has nice a little apartment on the second floor of her home. It can be RENT FREE, and maybe even come with a small salary! She's an older person with some memory problems and just needs a little help in the kitchen and keeping track of appointments. Would you like to meet her?"

"YES," Edna said, grimly. She'd promised God that she'd say YES for 24 hours, and the 24-hour period wasn't up yet.

"Could you meet her today? Could you stop in after work?

"YES," Edna forced herself to say. She wanted to say NO but she forced herself to say YES. And that was good enough for God.

Brother Flynn went on to explain Mrs. Kleine's condition but all Edna could do was sit and stare into space. She tried to listen and caught the gist of it. But Mrs. Kleine was in the *early stages* of Alzheimer's disease, Brother Flynn explained. Still largely independent she was content to live in her own home. She just couldn't live there alone anymore. "I'm afraid I'll have to meet you there," Brother Flynn apologized. "If you get there first just say you're a STUDENT and that you're looking for a room to rent. Just say you're a student."

"I'm a student," Edna said, robotically. "I'm a student." Edna missed part of the story but at least she got the gist of it. She looked down at the piece of paper with the address: 24 Eucalyptus Lane. Yes. After work. "Say I'm a student. Yes."

"Yes, that's great, Edna. See you there."

Chapter 22
"Mrs. Kleine's House'

Mrs. Kleine's house was a *modern* house, a modern split-level house built in 1950 and painted Sunshine Yellow. It was a stucco house. A few flowers languished in the front yard. Edna gathered her strength, walked up and rang the doorbell. No one seemed to be home. She started to walk away when she heard sounds of someone fiddling with the lock. "Coming! Coming," a voice rang out from within. "I'm having a little trouble with the door."

And finally, there was Mrs. Kleine, looking lovely in a beaded wool sweater and elegant black wool skirt even though it was warm out. Her white wavy hair brushed her shoulders lightly and framed her face. Wire rimmed glasses set off her sapphire blue eyes just SO.

"May I help you?" she smiled, surprised to find a stranger.

"Yes," Edna replied. "I'm here about the room?"

"The room?"

"I'm the ex-nun. Brother Flynn sent me?"

"I'm terribly sorry, but you see there is some kind of mix-up because I have always been Jewish."

"Oh, I mean--I'm a *student*," Edna lied, finally saying exactly what Brother Flynn told her to say. "I'm a friend of Brother Flynn. I'm looking for a room to rent. My name is Edna. I'm a student."

"Edna, what a lovely name," Mrs. Kleine smiled, feeling more relaxed. "Won't you come in?"

Edna followed Mrs. Kleine into the living room and looked around. This living room looked a lot like her mother's living room! The furniture looked like it had been purchased at the same department store in the same year, 1950. The Motorola TV Console looked just like her mother's. The *modern Scandinavian* coffee table looked almost identical, too. The only anomaly were the two comfy overstuffed chairs. The upholstery was getting worn out.

"This is my house and I like it. It's not as grand as the house in Dresden, but it's my house and I like it."

78

"Oh, it's a lovely house indeed," Edna said. "Brother Flynn said you had a room to rent, that you sometimes rented rooms to students?"

"Oh, yes. I have always enjoyed students. I used to be a German teacher, you know--a teacher of the German language. Won't you please come this way, and we can get acquainted."

Mrs. Kleine guided Edna through the living room and stopped in front of an old framed photo on the wall, a sepia portrait theatrically lit and turning dark around the edges, a portrait of a young woman with short, dark hair.

"I was Joan of Arc," Mrs. Kleine said.

"Joan of Arc?" Edna asked, startled. Were Mrs. Kleine's memory problems worse than Brother Flynn had told her? Did she really believe that she'd been St. Joan of Arc?

"Yes," Mrs. Kleine smiled. "I was Saint Joan."

"I see," Edna said. "You were Saint Joan?"

Mrs. Kleine believed she was St. Joan. It was more than Edna had bargained for, a woman who believe she was St. Joan. Edna tried to think of an excuse, any way to get out of there; but nothing came to her.

"Yes," Mrs. Kleine said, more emphatically. "I was Joan of Arc. I was Saint Joan--in the play by George Bernard Shaw, *Saint Joan*."

"Oh, you PLAYED Saint Joan--in the PLAY. How wonderful." Whew. Edna could finally relax.

"This photograph was taken by Genja Jonas, a very famous photographer in Berlin at that time. But I was never on stage in Berlin or even in Dresden. I was only in the *wander theater*. We pronounced it the *Vahn-Der-Tay-Ah-Ter*, but I'm sure you called it the *wander theater* here in America, didn't you?"

"I'm not certain," Edna replied.

"I know. Most people watch TV now. But we traveled all over the Rhineland, and sometimes the Ruhrland. We took the bus. How I loved it!"

"You were an actress in the theater! Wonderful! You will think I'm completely crazy, but it's my dream to go to Hollywood one day, and work in the film industry, as a writer."

"That is marvelous. You want to be an actress."

"No, I want to be a writer, in Hollywood!"

"You want to be a writer in Hollywood. That is also excellent, excellent! Well, what about a nice cup of coffee?"

Mrs. Kleine led Edna into the kitchen. Everything was *modern*. The table and chairs were white Formica with silver stars and chrome legs. The appliances were *avocado*. Mrs. Kleine stopped, and looked around.

"You know, it's the funniest thing. Sometimes I go into a room and I can't remember why, why I went into this room. It's the *darnedest* thing."

"That happens to everyone now and then."

"Yes, I suppose so," Mrs. Kleine said sadly. "But my memory is not what it was. When I was in the theater, I memorized so many lines! How did I ever do it? Well then, what about a cup of coffee, or maybe some ice cream?"

"Ah, ice cream! That would be lovely."

Mrs. Kleine was happy to open the freezer compartment of her Amanamatic Refrigerator. It was full of small paper cups of ice cream with small, flat wooden spoons attached to them. She reached in and handed one to Edna. "I'm afraid they're all chocolate, but they're quite good." And then they both enjoyed their ice cream, sitting together at Mrs. Kleine's kitchen table.

"Excuse me," Mrs. Kleine smiled at Edna, "but what did you say your name was?"

"Edna. ED-NA."

"Ah, Edna, a lovely name. Lovely."

"Thank you. Edna was a popular name once, but now Edna's are a dying breed, I'm afraid."

"Yes," Mrs. Kleine said. "Many people have died."

"Yes." For a few moments Edna had nothing else to say, but then she snapped out of it. "My last name is Reilly."

"Reilly, I see. What does it mean?"

"I don't know."

"My last name is *Kleine*, which means *small* in German. And my first name is *Bettina*, which means something like little *Betty*. That's me: *Little Betty Small!* Isn't that funny!"

That WAS funny. They both laughed. And then sounds of a car pulling up in front and Brother Flynn letting himself in with his own key.

"Hello! Is anybody here!" he called out, making his way thru the living room.

"Hello, Harold!" Mrs. Kleine called back. "We're in the kitchen!"

"OK! Ready or not, here I come!" Brother Flynn announced, cheerfully limping into the kitchen. "Well, I see you ladies have been getting acquainted! Hello Bettina! And Edna! I'm sorry to be late."

"Oh, Harold! You are not late," Mrs. Kleine replied.

Brother Flynn, known by Mrs. Kleine as *Harold*, plopped down into an empty kitchen chair and tried to make room under the table for his wooden leg. Mrs. Kleine brought him a little cup of ice cream with a tiny flat wooden spoon. When they were all nicely settled at the kitchen table, Brother Flynn orchestrated a few minutes of jovial conversation. Then he smiled and got a little notebook and a pen from a small canvas bag.

"OK then. Should we get started?"

"Why not?" Mrs. Kleine smiled. "What shall we start?"

"Well," Brother Flynn said, opening his ice cream cup, turning to Edna. "There are just a couple of things that Bettina sometimes could use some help with around the house--"

"Help! I need no help with *anything*," Mrs. Kleine interjected, insulted, "not at all!" The pleasant moment was shattered. Mrs. Kleine's face turned blank, a plain white oval with two shrunken blue dots of eyes in the middle.

"Well, maybe we can discuss it later." Brother Flynn managed, hoping to salvage the previously merry moment.

Mrs. Kleine was seriously offended. There was no turning back. Mrs. Kleine abruptly stood to face her *friend*.

"I think you'd better go, Harold!"

"All right. We can discuss this another day. Would you like a ride home, Edna?"

He stood up and looked helplessly at Edna. He tried to catch Edna's eye, nodding toward the front door. He wanted Edna to come

81

out and have a private chat for a minute, and assure her that all of this could (and would) easily be forgotten (and forgiven) soon. But Edna was perfectly happy where she was. In truth, she wanted to stay and finish her ice cream.

"No need to trouble yourself, Brother Flynn. I'll just catch the bus."

"Well, if you're sure," he replied, frowning and nodding his head toward the front door again.

Edna didn't take the hint. Brother Flynn (aka "Harold") made his way to the front door, limping along as he went, and let himself out, locking the door behind him. The sounds of Harold limping down the sidewalk to his car echoed on the pavement.

Mrs. Kleine took a deep breath and pushed her silvery-white hair back behind her ears, unveiling a lovely pair of small diamond earrings, which were attached to her ear lobes by little golden hoops. "My grandmother gave me these," she said, rubbing her ear lobes. They sat silently for a few moments. And then Mrs. Kleine spoke, slowly and clearly.

"I don't really need any help," she said gently, "but if *you need* a nice quiet room, I have several quiet rooms available upstairs. You'd like it here. It's nice and quiet!"

"How did she know?" Edna wondered.

Nice and quiet, that's exactly what she needed.

Chapter 23
"Edna's Dilemma"

Edna liked Mrs. Kleine, and her house was just a short walk from JSTB. If she moved in to Mrs. Kleine's house, she wouldn't have to take two buses to get to work! She was actually starting to feel cheerful again when Brother Flynn stopped at her desk.

"Did you decide what to do?"

"Yes. No more bus rides to work!"

"Of course not. If you lived at Mrs. Kleine's house, you'd already *be* at work."

"What do you mean? I would live there and work here. I'd only be working for Mrs. Kleine part-time, and at JSTB full-time." Perhaps it was not Edna's fault that she didn't quite understand the arrangement.

"Yes, of course you'd just be working at Mrs. Kleine's part-time," Brother Flynn explained, "but you'd still have to be there full-time, in case of emergency, but you could be upstairs working on your book. And the job comes with a salary, not a large one but so*mething*. You could save a little money. You won't have many expenses. You could work on your book!"

Mrs. Kleine was not an invalid nor was she an idiot. Edna saw no reason why she couldn't keep her job at JSTB, and help Mrs. Kleine after work and on weekends. But "No," Brother Flynn said, firmly but pleasantly. "Now she is still in the early stages; but she has Alzheimer's Disease. It's a *disease*, a progressive and eventually fatal illness. It changes over time. No one knows how much time."

Little by little the truth emerged. No, perhaps it was not Edna's fault that she'd misunderstood the situation. The deeper truth was that Mrs. Kleine did not need Edna to quit her job immediately and help her full-time; but Brother Flynn *did*. If he'd been brutally honest, Brother Flynn would have told her the truth but he didn't have the heart. The truth was that if she didn't quit her receptionist job voluntarily, she'd be *fired*, and it was up to him to help Edna out of an ugly scene.

"You got her in here; you can get her out," the Assistant Dean said. "This is your fault. You deal with it. Maybe something is wrong with her. Maybe she needs a doctor. Take her to the doctor. Take her to a rest home. Just take her away!"

Edna had no idea that anyone thought she was doing a poor job, or noticed how depressed she'd been feeling. Yes, she'd been doing a lot of staring into space, meditating and reading--but only when things were slow. Brother Flynn understood. When the serious professors, the Big Guns arrived for the Fall Semester, the real MEN IN BLACK would need someone FAST and CAPABLE, "not a charity case from a convent!" the Assistant Dean yelled. She had a powerful voice and wasn't afraid to use it. The next steps for Edna would be verbal and then written warnings with formal complaints, and then she'd be fired anyway. It would only make Edna feel worse.

"You could work on your book full-time," Brother Flynn pleaded. "I will find you a bevy of priests, ex-priests for you to interview, for your book, remember your book? I promise. It will all work out!"

"But I can't just leave JSTB like THAT. Can I?"

"Yes, you can. I'm THE FIXER, remember? I'll take care of it. And Former Father Tom is in desperate need of work. He's looking for a job as we speak. You'd be doing someone a good deed, simply by quitting your job!"

"But would the Jesuits hire someone who'd dropped out of their order?"

"Of course. We are not religious extremists."

"But what about insurance, and my week of vacation?" Edna was starting to learn to stand up for herself, drive a hard bargain.

"Oh, I'm sure that can be arranged. We can work it out." He wasn't sure, but he'd try.

"I need to sleep on it," Edna replied.

"Don't sleep too long," said Brother Flynn, and swished away, robes aflutter.

Edna's mother was starting a new life. Edna needed to start one, too, but she wasn't sure that living with Mrs. Kleine was a good first step. Many things could go wrong there. Mrs. Kleine was from a different generation, an older generation. There could be misunderstandings. She could interfere with her love life, if she ever had one. And she had a terminal illness. She could *die*. Edna tried to look at things from different points of view, things such as death. Death, on one hand it's a terrible thing, but on the other hand death was just a natural experience that happens to every living being. And Mrs. Kleine's illness WAS progressing slowly, very slowly. Before she died of Alzheimer's Disease, she could die of a heart attack or in an earthquake!

The next morning Edna went to work, opened up as usual, and then quit her job! Hallelujah! Everyone was happy, even Edna. She decided it was time for a change. She wasn't sure why. But she'd never been comfortable at JSTB, especially not in the cafeteria. *Former Father Tom* was happy. He'd have a full-time job, replacing Edna at the front desk. He needed it, a full-time job with benefits. He needed the health insurance. There wasn't a great demand for ex-priests over 60. Brother Flynn was happy because the Assistant Dean was happy. She even let him use a car to help Edna move. He helped Edna carry all of her things into Mrs. Kleine's house. Edna and Mrs. Kleine had to take it from there. He didn't do stairs well, not with his wooden leg, and foot.

Upstairs at Mrs. Kleine's Edna had a nice little bedroom, a nice little bathroom with her own little shower, and even a nice little library! It was a perfect place to write, a real God-send for any writer. It was like her own writers' colony right there at the edge of Holy Hill. There was a perfect desk, a perfect reading lamp, and a comfy little couch! Shelves of books covered most of the wall space, kind of like the Lounge at JSTB in miniature. Edna luxuriated in the silence and the books. And many of them were in English. And then she went downstairs to visit Mrs. Kleine.

"Wow, you have a lot of books," Edna exclaimed as she walked back down the stairs into the living room. One stair squeaked.

"I should fix that stair one day," Mrs. Kleine reminded herself. "But yes, I have many wonderful books. Many students have come to live here through the years and left their books behind. You know, I was once a teacher of the German language but students who stayed here studied many languages. And what will you be studying?"

"Priests," Edna replied, "ex-priests."

"Ex-priests, that is fascinating," Mrs. Kleine exclaimed.

"Such drama! Before I became a teacher of the German language, I was an actress. How I loved the stage! I memorized so many lines. How did I ever do it? My memory is not so good any more. But I loved it, I loved the stage."

Chapter 24
"Afternoon Movie Classic"

Alzheimer's Disease is a *progressive disease,* a *degenerative disease.* It goes in stages. One of the stages is marked by dementia but Mrs. Kleine wasn't demented. She was just forgetful, and sometimes watched too much TV.

"I like TV," she mentioned to Edna as they watched an afternoon soap opera. "My second husband didn't want me to watch daytime TV. He wanted me to cook and clean and be a normal wife. Let's just see what else is on, shall we?"

"Good idea." Edna had never seen a soap opera before. Her mother never liked them.

This one was terrible so they turned to another one. Mrs. Kleine started to enjoy it. Edna went upstairs to look through books. A copy of "Sanctuary" by William Faulkner popped out. Edna *tried* to read it but kept getting mixed up. Who was talking? Who were they talking to? Edna gave up and headed back downstairs to see what was on TV. On her way down she stepped on that squeaky stair, the one that always squeaked when you stepped on it. It didn't seem to be broken, just squeaky.

"I should fix that stair one day!" Mrs. Kleine called out, "but the Movie Classic is about to begin. Care to join me?"

"Thanks!" Edna said, making herself comfortable. "What's on?"

"A movie." She didn't really know which movie. It didn't matter. It was the Afternoon Movie Classic, though, that much she knew. "Won't you have a chocolate?" She passed Edna the box of Thin Mints.

"Thanks!"

Edna unwrapped her Thin Mint just in time for a commercial. A slice of pizza appeared on screen, singing and doing a cha-cha. Pizza. Cha-cha-cha. Pizza. Cha-cha-cha. Then, the slice of pizza danced away.

"You know, when I was on stage," Mrs. Kleine mentioned, "we had costumes and scenery; but nothing like *this*." She pointed to the vanishing slice of pizza, and swished her fingers through the air with a grand flourish.

"Didn't you ever want to go to Hollywood?" Edna asked, as a cigarette commercial followed.

"I did go to Hollywood," Mrs. Kleine recalled. "I went with my second husband. We went to Grauman's Chinese Theater."

"But did you ever want to go to Hollywood and act in films?"

"When we came to America, I had to learn English fast and I had an accent."

The movie starred John Wayne and Maureen O'Hara in "The Quiet Man." But it wasn't a Western; it took place in Ireland. Mrs. Kleine and Edna both liked it. When it was over Mrs. Kleine went up to the desk in her room and made a note in her journal, her Life Book:

"Saw *Quiet Man* with lovely new student who lives upstairs. Wonderful film, a real delight!"

And then Edna fixed supper, sliced chicken sandwiches with avocado and lettuce and Kosher dill pickles, just like her mother used to make. It happened to be one of Mrs. Kleine's favorite meals, too, and required no cooking. After dinner they cleared away their plates and washed the dishes. Edna kept thinking about Hollywood. Mrs. Kleine never wanted to go to Hollywood. She had enough on her plate, escaping from the Nazis.   Edna asked her again, though, beginning to *pester*. Mrs. Kleine didn't mind. She couldn't remember what Edna just said.

"But when you came to America, did you think about going to Hollywood, to act in films?" Edna asked again, just to re-check.

"No," she said. When she came to America, she had to learn English fast and had an accent. No, she did not think about going to Hollywood to be in the movie industry. But Edna did.

Chapter 25
"Breakfast"

Edna's duties included helping with the grocery shopping and meal preparation. It was easy. Mrs. Kleine liked eating the same thing every day. For breakfast, Cheerios and banana slices, juice, and instant coffee with milk. Why did breakfast take two hours? Edna wondered. But everything went slowly at Mrs. Kleine's house, which left ample time to share stories, mostly Mrs. Kleine's stories of yesteryear:

... My second husband, Arnold Kleine, was an awful man. Awful. He always criticized me and my cooking and the way I cleaned the house. Sometimes I would try to tell him that I was not the maid, after all; but he would merely criticize me further.

"Too bad," Edna would commiserate.

Shopping for groceries proved to be easy. Happily, there was a small grocery store with a nice little deli just two blocks away on Euclid Avenue, The Good Food Store. There were bigger, cheaper grocery stores down in "The Flatlands" in downtown Berkeley, but it was too far to walk. The Good Food Store cost extra but considering bus or taxi fare, it cost the same and saved aggravation.

Edna and Mrs. Kleine kept it simple. And whatever Edna prepared, Mrs. Kleine always said "Marvelous, absolutely marvelous!" She never criticized Edna's *cooking*, unlike her second husband:

... My second husband, Arnold Kleine, was an awful man. Awful. He always criticized me and my cooking and..."

After a few days or maybe a few weeks, I was hard to tell, Edna and Mrs. Kleine began to get used to each other. Edna wondered why she hadn't heard from Brother Flynn. She'd hoped he might think of another ex-priest for her to interview.

Chapter 26
"Lunch and Dinner"

Alzheimer's Disease is a strange disease. You couldn't even be certain that someone had it. The only conclusive test, then, was autopsy. But you didn't need a test to know what was happening to Mrs. Kleine. She was forgetting too many things. But she never forgot how mean her second husband was:

"My second husband Arnold Kleine was so mean that he died standing up. Yes, standing up! He was so mean that he wouldn't even lie down and die. I went to temple that morning as usual. It was a Saturday morning. When I came home, I heard nothing, just silence. And then I went into the kitchen to have a nice cup of coffee and there he was, standing in the doorway dead as a doornail! He was so mean that he would not even lie down and die."

And if Mrs. Kleine lost her reading glasses over and over, and came up to pester Edna more and more often, at least Mrs. Kleine was nice about it, which is more than you can say for some people who don't even have a disease at all. Take a healthy young person who has lost his or her glasses.

"Shit," he or she might say, "I can't find my fucking glasses!"

"Please excuse me," Mrs. Kleine would say very politely, "but I can't find my glasses. I wonder if you've seen them anywhere?"

There was plenty of space for both of them in the house. If Mrs. Kleine got on Edna's nerves more and more because she was losing things more and more, at least they were not tripping over each other. And when Mrs. Kleine came upstairs to pester Edna because she lost something, at least she was polite about it. And they always had sandwiches for lunch and dinner. It was easy to fix and easy to digest. Sometimes Edna made spaghetti with tomato sauce. Everyone likes spaghetti and it was easy to make. They had it in the convent often-- with meatballs, or just with tomato sauce, sometimes only with olive oil and grated cheese, and/or fresh basil from their garden.   In the evenings Edna and Mrs. Kleine often liked to watch TV together.

90

"I enjoy TV," Mrs. Kleine remarked. It was time for a commercial. A tube of toothpaste sang and danced. This toothpaste would give your mouth that clean, fresh feeling. It would give your mouth *Sex Appeal*! During the commercial break, Mrs. Kleine went off to the kitchen to find a snack. She couldn't remember what she was looking for. She returned empty handed but settled back into her chair and happily opened the box of Thin Mints sitting there on the coffee table, just in time. And if Mrs. Kleine hadn't been interested in going to Hollywood, Edna was. But she had to keep some of these thoughts to herself. She had to quit bugging Mrs. Kleine.

"Did you never try acting in films?" Edna asked, again. She couldn't help it. She thought she'd give it a try once more. Just in case Mrs. Kleine might remember something new.

"No," she had never tried acting in films though. She was quite certain. She was "only in the wander theater and that was the traveling theater. I was happy but my parents were unhappy, very unhappy. But what about you? Do you want to go to Hollywood and act in films?"

"Well, I'm hoping to complete three books and get them published, and then go to Hollywood."

"Ah, you wish to become a screen writer!"

"Yes, I know it's ridiculous."

"No! It is marvelous, absolutely marvelous! You must go to Hollywood. But first you must find an agent. My grandmother introduced me to my agent. She used to have *salons*, wonderful parties and she invited many talented people, actors and directors and artists and musicians. And me! She invited me! That's where I met my agent. What you need is the right agent."

"Well, first I have to finish my first book."

"I see. And what is your book about?"

"Priests, ex-priests."

"Ex-priests. That is marvelous, absolutely marvelous! You know, when I was in the theater, I had a lover. His name was Boris, and he played the villains! He was a BIG WHEEL in the theater company. He was so gifted, so talented. His German was even better than mine, and he was Russian! He played the frightening roles. How do you say it? Ah. I know: the villains. He played the villains, and that was before I got married."

"I was only married to Christ, I'm afraid," Edna mentioned. "I was in the convent for almost twelve years. I took a vow of poverty, and so now I have nothing. I did get my dowry back. But it was only $200, and I owed it to my mother."

"Twelve years, that's a long time."

"It didn't seem like it at the time. I used to love the convent. I loved singing with the choir. I could sing with the choir every day!"

"I understand. My first job on the stage was with the chorus. I loved it! You must start somewhere. Start in the chorus, go out into the world and find a new lover! You never know who you might meet."

Chapter 27
"Reading to the Blind"

Edna was well suited to her job at Mrs. Kleine's. She was very good at keeping track of Mrs. Kleine's appointments. There were only two:
Friday, Reading to the Blind (9-11:30am)
Saturday, Hadassah Sisterhood (9:30-11am)

One day was like the next. First thing every morning Mrs. Kleine opened her front door and got her newspaper, her *San Francisco Chronicle* from the front steps. Then she and Edna had breakfast, read the paper and chatted. Then Mrs. Kleine carefully folded up each newspaper and put it on a pile with other newspapers from that week. On Fridays she put all of them into two shopping bags and took them over to her neighbor Dr. Q. who was blind. Mrs. Kleine had met him long ago when she volunteered for Reading to the Blind.

"It's Friday," Mrs. Kleine announced to Edna early that morning. "It's time for Reading to the Blind. Would you like to come?"

"Thank you, no. I haven't had a cup of coffee yet," Edna replied. It was true. She'd only had HALF a cup.

"Dr. Q always prepares coffee and he is a very special person. Oh yes, very special indeed. And he lives very close by, not far at all. It's very easy to get there. Why don't you come?"

Edna couldn't think of any other excuse to get out of it. And so, she went along. And as it turned out Dr. Q *didn't* live that far away at all, just next door. He lived in a small brick apartment building right next door, on the first floor, and it was very easy to get there. You just had to walk across Mrs. Kleine's front yard and go in the back entrance. When they arrived, Dr. Q was waiting for them in his doorway, holding a white cane and wearing dark glasses.

He was about 4'10" and weighed about 90 pounds, maybe. He had a thin patch of silvery white hair combed neatly over to one side, and silvery white eyebrows to match, forming little awnings over his dark glasses. His clothes were all beige.

"Welcome Bettina! And Edna, is it?"

"Yes, yes, it's Edna," Edna chimed back.

"I've been hoping to meet you! Please, won't you come in?"

"Oh, thank you so much," Edna replied politely. She had little choice. Too late to turn back now.

There were books and papers everywhere, piled up on coffee tables. But he ushered them to two empty seats, and sat down on the third.

"Yes," he said to Edna. "I can guess at what you are thinking. I have many books and papers, that is true. My name is Alfred Quedresque--but everyone calls me *Dr. Q,* only because I have an honorary degree from the North Berkeley Community College! Of course, it is only a joke. The Community College offers no PhD's!"

Edna could not help but stare at him. And his clothes. They were all beige.

"And you are probably wondering why everything I am wearing is beige," he smiled at Edna. "That is so everything will go together. No need to match colors!" That made sense. She looked around, at all the books and papers, spilling out of file cabinets and stacked up in every empty space. But nothing in Braille. Once more he seemed to read Edna's mind. "Yes, I have many books but none of them in Braille," he said. "I never learned Braille. As you can see, I am blind; but I have not always been blind. I became blind later in life and so I never learned Braille."

The coffee table in front of them was covered with clips from newspaper articles, piles of them, and essays. He'd written all of them. Some of the pages had turned yellow with age. The one on top was number #727. It was the last article he wrote before retiring. He'd put a little notch in the upper left-hand corner, dog-eared, so he could identify it by touch. It was entitled *Baden Saison Mit Schrecht, or, Fear and Trembling in the Swimming Season.* Again, it was as if he intuited her thoughts.

"Yes, that one closest to you was about sharks. #727. Normally they don't bother anyone."

"I typed that article," Mrs. Kleine interjected, "and I strongly disagree. Sharks are a very dangerous type of fish.

94

"I SAID normally. Normally they don't hurt humans. I wanted people to *understand* sharks not just fear them."

And then it was time for coffee. They hadn't *taken* their coffee yet. Slowly and carefully he reached for his cane and led them into the *kitchenette*. "It's only a kitchenette," he explained, tapping his way long, "but I prefer such. Everything is within easy reach."

The kitchenette was small but with just enough room for three folding chairs and a little café table. Everything was spare and tidy. Mrs. Kleine and Edna got situated at the table. Dr. Q ran his fingers along one of the cabinet doors and opened it. The cups, sugar, instant coffee and instant creamer were all there, in a row. He got everything out and added a spoonful of instant coffee granules and some warm tap water to each cup. Edna offered to help boil some water, but no. She was his guest. He wanted to serve HER. And the water couldn't be too hot. Being blind, he might spill some and burn himself. Each person could add sugar and/or creamer if desired. And then he joined them at the table. "Ah coffee, so good!" Mrs. Kleine exclaimed. Edna agreed. It almost was.

"You know, my grandmother and I used to go to Vienna, all the way from Dresden to Vienna, just for cake and coffee. We took the train. Ah, the cakes in Vienna! And the coffee, it was nothing like *this*." She looked down at her cup, sadly.

"Mrs. Kleine, that's rude!" Edna blurted out. She didn't usually blurt things out but she felt bad for Dr. Q, insulting his coffee after he worked so hard to make it. But he didn't seem to be offended.

"I know, Bettina. The cakes and the coffee in Vienna were much better." And then turned to speak to Edna. "When I was younger, I lived in Vienna. It was very beautiful and very rich culturally. In Vienna I was a magazine publisher. We published articles about The East. But in the 30's I had to sell everything and get out."

"I'm sorry to hear that, Dr. Q," Edna said. "At least you got out." She tapped his hand lightly. Usually she kept her hands to herself. But Dr. Q just kept talking.

"I was born in Romania but I was just one of 300,000 Romanian Jews who were not even considered to be Romanian citizens. Even those of us who were born there were treated as foreigners in our own country and could be expelled at any time, for any reason."

95

"That's terrible!" Edna said.

"Yes, absolutely terrible," Mrs. Kleine agreed.

"Before WWI I was a pacifist. I was arrested for my pacifism and put in jail in Romania but was released under the condition that I leave the country."

"And did you leave the country?" Mrs. Kleine asked.

"Yes, of course I left the country. You know that! I went to Vienna. But there was nothing else of interest about my life in Romania."

That was quite a story, possibly the beginning of an entire book. Maybe God wanted her to write a book about him! But then it was time to start reading the newspaper.

"Yes," Mrs. Kleine and Dr. Q agreed. "Let's get started, shall we?" They only had *a couple of hours*.

They finished their coffee and returned to the living room. Mrs. Kleine got a newspaper out of her tote bag and began reading headlines. After all, it was Reading to the Blind Day. She started at the top of the front page, a story about government corruption, and went on to an article about Paul Robeson singing in Moscow. He was a highly acclaimed singer, a bass baritone, but he went to Moscow to sing. Some Americans called him a "Communist."

"Good for him," Dr. Q said.

After reading the front-page headlines, Mrs. Kleine turned to the Entertainment Section. "Let's see if there's a new movie out!" She turned immediately to the Arts and Entertainment section.

"Yes," Dr. Q and Edna agreed.

Dr. Q wanted to go back and hear the whole story about Paul Robeson singing in Moscow. Mrs. Kleine had to put the Entertainment Section on hold. An hour later they had finished reading and discussing the articles in the first newspaper and were ready to go onto the second newspaper. The next one went a little faster. They didn't stop to discuss everything. Sometimes Mrs. Kleine just read the headlines.

And then it was time to go. By the time they got back home most of the morning was over. Edna felt tired somehow.

Chapter 28
"Hadassah Sisterhood!"

It was Saturday. Edna and Mrs. Kleine got up and had breakfast. And then Mrs. Kleine got ready to walk to her Hadassah meeting. There was going to be a special presentation on the Yiddish Language. Mrs. Kleine had read an article about it in the newspaper. It was the first day of "Celebrate Yiddish Week" in Berkeley. It was also a nice foggy morning, a nice morning to go back to bed, Edna thought. But what about Mrs. Kleine? Would she be OK walking by herself? Would she get lost? Would she forget the way? Maybe it would be interesting!

"Would you like some company?" Edna sked.

"Oh no," Mrs. Kleine said firmly. "I always walk by myself to Hadassah every Saturday. And besides, you are not Jewish." And off she went.

No, Edna was not Jewish but she wondered how Mrs. Kleine knew that. They'd never discussed religion very much at all. But it was fine with Edna because she didn't want to go anywhere. Mrs. Kleine went out to her meeting and Edna went upstairs to look at books. So many books! Edna selected a copy of *The Collected Works of Edgar Allan Poe* and went back to bed to read.

It was a sleepy morning. Edna had no idea how long she'd been asleep, or even realize that she HAD been asleep. Suddenly there came a-rapping, rap-tap-tapping, tapping at her chamber door. It was Mrs. Kleine, back from her Hadassah Sisterhood meeting early. Only this, nothing more.

"Excuse me," she said, "but I cannot find Harold's telephone number."

"How was your meeting, or lecture was it?"

"Terrible! They spoke Yiddish!"

"But I thought it was about Yiddish, wasn't it?"

"Yes, the poor people, they spoke Yiddish!"

"But the lecture was about Yiddish, the Yiddish language."

"Yes," Mrs. Kleine agreed. "It was terrible. And so, I left."

"Ah, that's too bad."

"Yes, too bad."

Mrs. Kleine went downstairs to call Harold, but she kept dialing the wrong number. After a series of wrong numbers, she went back up to see Edna again.

"It's the darnedest thing. I'm terribly sorry to bother you but I can't seem to find Harold's number. I wonder if you have it?"

"I'll look."

Edna found Harold's phone number and wrote it down in large numbers on a piece of paper and taped it to the wall over the telephone, and returned to *The Collected Works of Edgar Allan Poe*. Perhaps fifteen minutes later she heard a gentle rapping, rap-tap-tapping, again. It was Mrs. Kleine, tapping at her chamber door. She still couldn't find Harold's number. "I am trying to call Harold," she said, sadly, "but I cannot find his number."

Mrs. Kleine was anxious about something. She was having a bad morning, only this, nothing more. Edna felt bad that she hadn't gone with her, but looking on the good side, at least Mrs. Kleine found her way back home! Edna wrote down Harold's phone number in Magic Marker on a large piece of paper, and taped it to the wall over the phone. Plain as day, no one could miss it. Mrs. Kleine was worried about something, though, and she hadn't seen *Harold* in a while. What happened to him? What about their coffee appointment?

Edna always did her best to be helpful to Mrs. Kleine, and so she called *Harold* herself. Harold agreed to have coffee with Mrs. Kleine every Wednesday at 9:45 am. He picked that time because there was a lecture on poetry every Wednesday at 10 at the Berkeley Public Library, done by someone in the community. Mrs. Kleine jotted it down on the Wednesday square on her calendar: "coffee with Harold, 9:45. Poetry Lecture at Berkeley Public Library, and coffee at Downtown Coffee Shop!" Mrs. Kleine didn't especially like poetry but she liked Downtown Coffee Shop, and so she would go.

While she had Brother Flynn ("Harold") on the phone that day, Edna took the opportunity to ask him about her project. Any more ex-priests for her to interview? Not this week, sorry. His hands were full trying to train Former Father Tom at the front desk; the Fall Semester had started and it was a bumpy ride. Edna was vindicated. That job wasn't as easy as you might think. When things were finally under control Brother Flynn would see what he could do. OK, thanks! And true to his word, on Wednesday morning Brother Flynn drove over to Mrs. Kleine's house to pick her up. He was using a borrowed Jesuit car. She was all ready and waiting at the door so he wouldn't have to go to the trouble of adjusting his wooden leg, get out and limp up to the front door and then limp back to the car again. He could just toot the horn and she'd dash out. Off they went. Whoosh! Bye-bye!

Left alone in peace and quiet, Edna made another selection from Mrs. Kleine's bookshelves, *Swan's Way* by Marcel Proust and made herself comfortable on the couch in the study. She loved page one but by the end of page two her eyelids began to get heavy. She must have dozed off. When she woke up, she heard someone downstairs. It was Mrs. Kleine stomping around the house, looking for matches so she could light the stove and make coffee. The matches had vanished.

Edna went to the corner store for matches. When she returned the house was very quiet. She went up to the mezzanine level to look for Mrs. Kleine. She was in her room. Her door was open. She had a nice pleasant room with clean white curtains, a comfy bed and a nice big desk. She was busy at her desk writing something in a little notebook.

"Oh, please come in. I was just writing in my Life Book," she smiled, "it's like a diary but it's not private. Anyone may read it." She moved aside so Edna could read over her shoulder:

"Terrible class! Yiddish poetry, with Harold! I walked back!"

It was *Celebrate Yiddish* Week in Berkeley. But as it turned out, Mrs. Kleine didn't enjoy Yiddish. Too bad. Oh well. And then it was time for everyone to cheer up and have a nice cup of coffee and a little conversation.

"You know, sometimes I used to stay with my grandmother and that was when my mother was ill. My grandmother had a big, beautiful house in Dresden, a beautiful house with lots of marvelous paintings, a real Monet!"

Just then the phone rang. It was Harold! He had found an ex-priest for Edna to interview! "He lives right here on Holy Hill, and would be delighted to come over and speak with you. He's free this

Sunday afternoon around 2. Would that be ok?" Yes! Yes, that would be great.

Chapter 29
"Communication"

On Sunday afternoon Edna cleaned off the dining room table and got ready for her next *interview*. Former Father Michael would arrive in 15 minutes! Mrs. Kleine was in the living room studying her *TV Guide*, checking the listings for the afternoon when Dr. Q called. He wanted to know if Edna and Mrs. Kleine wanted to take a little walk to the Good Food Store. He needed some bread and they had his favorite rye bread at the deli. Edna was going to be busy, sorry, but she put Mrs. Kleine on the line. Moments later Mrs. Kleine grabbed her purse and set out.

"Have a lovely time!" Edna said. "Will you be OK walking there?"

"Oh yes, I often take Dr. Q to buy bread. He has the good memory and I have the good eyes!"

"Are you sure you don't need me?"

"We will be just fine. We shall. We will, we shall. I have the good eyes and he has the good memory!"

Dr. Q had home health aide who did most of his shopping, laundry, and house cleaning regularly. But if he wanted simply to go out, maybe to the Good Food Store, he sometimes called Mrs. Kleine. Every time Dr. Q called, Mrs. Kleine dropped whatever she was doing, rushed over to Dr. Q's apartment and guided him to wherever he wanted to go, often to the Good Food Store deli. Sometimes she found a nice apple turnover or an éclair. Sometimes they stopped for coffee.

Edna had the whole house to herself and was ready to greet Former Father Michael. They got started right away. Tea? No, thanks, no tea. He launched right in. Edna took notes.

"Interview #2 with Former Father Michael"
(as told to Edna Reilly)

"I was a career man in the Navy. Everyone in the service hates it. I was no exception. It was the beginning of the Cold War. I was on The Tunny. It was maybe 1953. And we were carrying nuclear cruise missiles. Most people didn't realize we had them then. Not like the Big Guns they had later, not like on the Nautilus but we had 'em. Anyway, you'd think: 'I could blow up a million people, or get blown up.' I can still hear the sounds, the pings. Bip-bip-bip. We had all the latest stuff--the radar, the sonar. The Russians were never far away and were we scared! I always had the feeling that we could get blown up, or blow plenty of other people up. It was a crisis of nerves. I'd sit there and listen to that bip-bip-bip, that ping-ping-ping...

It was DEATH, fear of DEATH. Nobody talked about it, about Death, but everyone knew. It was always there, waiting. Sometimes when there was nothing to do, just to get my mind off it I read books. I think I read every book on the ship. I must have read a hundred books. I checked them out of the Charleston, South Carolina public library when we got into port. They gave me as many as I wanted. I was good for it. We always came up for air in Charleston.

I loved Charleston. But in the back of my mind it was always there, DEATH, waiting in the wings. I always that the feeling that we could get blown up any day. I read and read but I was still scared to die. Bip-bip-bip. The sound was always there, just to remind you. I made a deal with God that if I ever got off of that sub alive, I'd enter the priesthood.

So, I got out of that sub alive and after I got off the sub and out of the Navy, I kept my promise to God. I went straight into the priesthood. I wasn't fooling around. I joined Franciscan Friars.

At the novitiate they saw how scared of death I was. The Franciscans saw that, and so they sent me to hospitals and nursing homes to work. Did I see death in hospitals and nursing homes! Over and over for years. I gave last rites so many times I finally got bored. I guess it helped me with my fear of dying. I hope I was able to help some other people, people who were dying, or grieving or just plain scared of death, like ME. I finally got bored. It took a long time but finally I got bored with death. It was like I woke up and wanted to explore living again!

And no, I didn't leave the priesthood because of sex. Everyone wants to know, but most people are too polite to ask. No. I know it's a problem for many priests in The Church, but I just never encountered it myself. For me it was all about death. One day I just got my love of LIFE back, and wasn't afraid of DEATH any more. Many people can't face even the thought of DEATH, but once you do your life will be a lot happier. Mine did."

Before he left, Former Father Michael told Edna about some of his experiences with people who had Alzheimer's disease. He'd seen it over and over in nursing homes and hospitals. "The damage it does is really something," he said, and shook his head. "I hope you're going to get some extra help around here. You'll need it, sooner or later."

And then he had to go. He was meeting his wife for dinner. Too bad. Edna kind of liked him. After he left, Edna made herself a cup of tea and checked Mrs. Kleine's *TV Guide* to see what was on. She wasn't worried about Mrs. Kleine or Dr. Q. The Good Food Store was only two and a half blocks away.

"This is the way we go," Mrs. Kleine said, taking him cheerfully by the elbow, ushering him down the hallway, out the door and around the corner to Euclid Ave.

"Thank you," he said, as pleasantly as he could.

It took Mrs. Kleine and Dr. Q over an hour to get there. Dr. Q bought a loaf of marbled rye bread, sliced, and a chocolate éclair. Mrs. Kleine bought nothing.

"This cake is wrong," Mrs. Kleine commented, acidly, looking at the cakes in the deli case.

"How can a cake be wrong?" Dr. Q asked, patiently. "People are wrong, not cakes."

"But these cakes are all wrong!"

"Was ist loss mit eine Kleine apfel Kuchen, Bettina?" he asked.

"The cakes in Vienna were much better."

"Yes," he agreed, "of course the cakes in Vienna were better, but you are not in Vienna! *Mas wir sind nicht jetz in Wein*! We are in Berkeley! We must learn to be satisfied with Euclid Bakery!"

They were on their way home when Mrs. Kleine remembered that she forgot something. She needed to go back. She forgot her Thin

Mints and her avocado and so they turned back. Mrs. Kleine picked up her Thin Mints and an avocado. She liked avocados very much. And then it was time to go home.

"Maybe we should take a cab back," Mrs. Kleine suggested on the way back. "We could get back in a jiffy."

"I do not want to get back in a jiffy," Dr. Q replied, sternly. "I want to walk."

They started to walk but got only a few steps from the Good Food Store when Mrs. Kleine got in the mood for a cup of coffee. "What about a little cup of coffee at Euclid Café? It's right here, I believe."

"Ah, Euclid Café, wonderful! Yes, let's stop!"

And they did. At the Euclid Café they enjoyed de-caf coffee and cookies, and a little light conversation, at first about the weather. And then Mrs. Kleine began reminiscing about her life in the theater.

"… but no, I was never on stage in Vienna or even in Dresden. I was only in the wander theater. But the theater, how I loved it!"

"The Weimar Republic, it was built on egg shells. We knew it wouldn't last."

"No, it didn't last. And then no Jewish actresses could be on stage. But I loved Brecht, and Shaw!"

"Yes, the theater was nice. But what good was the theater when we were up against the Nazis! Some of us fought Hitler, you know. We were socialists and communists and we fought him!" He was starting to lose his patience. It was time to go. They dropped the subject and started their return journey home. They didn't have far to go, just a couple of blocks but it was starting to get dark out. The days were getting shorter.

"Why is this taking so long?" Dr. Q asked, eventually. "Do you see a street sign?"

"No sign but it looks like… it could be Eucalyptus. I'm not sure."

Their happy mood was gone. Mrs. Kleine tried to recapture a happy memory as she reminisced again about her life in Germany during the early 1930's and her life in the theater.

"Yes, I was in the wander theater. My favorite play was *Saint Joan* by George Bernard Shaw. I had the lead role, the starring role!"

"But you were never in the Yiddish Theater," he replied. "I loved the Yiddish Theater, the Yiddish language, Yiddish literature!"

"The Yiddish theater! The poor people of The Pale," she went on, unfortunately. "They came with their bundles and their children."

"You people had it easy till we arrived."

"Yes," she agreed, "it was terrible and they spoke YIDDISH."

"I MYSELF was a poor person who spoke Yiddish," he retorted.

"I didn't mean YOU. But the poor, poor people from The Pale. They spoke *Yiddish*."

"And you spoke 'High German' and you felt *superior*."

"Oh, yes," she agreed, happy once again. "I was raised on High German and we were superior, absolutely. I had the starring role in *Saint Joan*, by George Bernard Shaw."

"Shaw!" *he* retorted. He was tired. He'd had enough. Enough of the trip to the Good Food Store and the Euclid Café, and surely enough of Mrs. Kleine. "What do you know of Shaw? George Bernard Shaw was a socialist! He believed in something! When he received the Nobel Prize, he shared it with other writers. George Bernard Shaw believed in something. He believed in the redistribution of wealth. What do you believe in?"

"Believe, believe," she said, wracking her brain, trying to think of an answer to his question, trying to think of what she believed. Finally, she had it. "I believe we are Jewish. Yes, I am sure of it. I believe I am Jewish. I believe we are Jews."

"I am sorry, Bettina. Please forgive an old man, just an old man, lost in the dark."

When Edna finally found them, it wasn't dark yet but it was starting to get dark. She found them just around the corner. Edna and Mrs. Kleine walked Dr. Q to his apartment and went then they went home, too. Mrs. Kleine was exhausted. She went up to her room to relax and make an entry in her Life Book:

"Terrible trip to Éclair Bakery with Dr. Q! He hates me! Thank God I still have Harold!"

"I like TV," Mrs. Kleine said after she recuperated from her walk to the deli.

"I do, too!" Edna agreed.

Mrs. Kleine got out her *TV Guide* to see what was on, and Edna turned on the TV. It was the October Fest Film Festive, German movies! The first movie was an old black and white film in German with subtitles. It was half over but they decided to watch it anyway and tried to catch up. It was morning rush hour, as employees were entering the lobby of an office building, mostly women. Time for work! There were several elevators but most of the workers were walking up a beautiful marble and wrought iron and marble staircase. The few people riding up in the elevators were men in three-piece suits.

"I don't get it," Edna said. "A couple of people are taking the elevators. Everyone else is walking up."

"It was the same in my father's chemical company," Mrs. Kleine recalled. "Only the BIG SHOTS got to ride in the elevator. Everyone else had to walk."

The next morning Mrs. Kleine was still thinking about her father as she lingered over her coffee.

"My father was a good father, I must say. He got up with me every morning and had breakfast with me. Then he was chauffeured to the chemical factory, and I walked to school. He didn't want the other children to see me arrive in a limousine. And he didn't want me to be spoiled. He just wanted me to get some exercise and be a regular kid and I was. I was a regular kid and I walked to school."

"I walked to my elementary school, too I was a regular kid, too, and so I walked."

"I did, too," Mrs. Kleine added.

"I started out in public school but later I went to Catholic school."

"I went to the customary school and studied the customary subjects; but when it was time for religion classes the Jewish students had to go to a special room. And sometimes girls in my class had parties

106

and didn't invite me. Even then some people wanted 'no Jewish influence.' That's the way they put it, *no Jewish influence*."

Chapter 30
"Edna (Almost) Gives Up"

When Mrs. Kleine returned from her Hadassah meeting, she tried to walk into the kitchen and make a cup of coffee but Edna was in her way. Edna was scrubbing the kitchen floor, wearing that same gray cotton dress her mother used to wear when she cleaned the house. Mrs. Kleine stood there for a minute. She thought that Edna was talking to her. But Edna was talking to herself, mumbling unhappily.

"Excuse me," Mrs. Kleine said. "Is something wrong?"

"My writing is going nowhere," Edna said, tragically.

"Where do you want it to go?"

"I don't know! My writing has no dramatic arc!"

"Of course, the dramatic arc!" Mrs. Kleine replied. "The dramatic arc is the key to an entire drama. I understand completely. You are trying to write a drama and you are suffering from writer's block."

"Is that it?" Edna said. She stopping scrubbing, stunned at this revelation, and looked up to find Mrs. Kleine. "But how did you know?"

"I've seen it before with writers in the theater. Do you have a deadline?"

"Oh," Edna said, embarrassed. "No, I have no deadline."

"What does your agent say? Have you called your agent?"

"Well," said Edna, and then she dropped her scrub brush, stood up and took a deep breath. God was Edna's agent and God was proving to be unreliable. "In fact," Edna confessed at long length, "I don't really have an agent at all. My wish to go to Hollywood is nothing but a dream. All I have is a dream, just a dream to tell you the truth and I just give up."

"Don't give up on your dreams!" Mrs. Kleine begged. "Never, never give up on your dreams! After all, 'Aller anfant ist schwer,' It's an old Deutsche sprichtwort, an old saying. 'All beginnings are hard.' Sometimes one must wait. Inspiration will come. You'll see."

Edna waited for several days and began again to sink into listlessness, into depression. It was breakfast time but Edna didn't feel like eating. More real estate agents were going to be coming through her mother's house in El Cerrito. She didn't care. She just sat there on a kitchen chair. Mrs. Kleine successfully found some matches and lit a burner on the stove. The water was just come to a boil when the phone rang. It was Brother Flynn (Harold). He had another ex-priest for Edna to interview. He just happened to be at JSTB right now and would be willing to come over and talk with you now.

"Is now a good time for Jim to come over and talk to you?"

"Yes, yes it would be a fine time!" Edna said. "Thank you!"

Edna had some instant coffee, not de-caf, and tried to rally for her next interview! Her next interview was with a person named James but people called him Jim or Jimmy. This ex-priest used to be a Franciscan. Edna was delighted. She'd always been curious about the Franciscans. They took their vow of poverty seriously, as Brother Flynn had told her. Quickly Edna put her cleaning supplies away and prepared the dining room table for the interview. Mrs. Kleine made herself comfortable in the living room watching TV, just anything.

When Jimmy arrived, they chatted about poverty and Hollywood. And then they got started. Edna's interview went something like this:

"Interview #3 with Former Father Jim
A Franciscan's Story"
(as told to Edna Reilly)

"I'm just a typical American man in many ways. For me it was always about heroes. My hero was St. Francis. Other men joined the Franciscans for that same exact reason. He was a different kind of male hero, a man who could inspire us. He was my hero, absolutely. I asked to join the Franciscan Friars. Every Catholic religious order is founded by a saint. The Franciscans were founded by St. Francis, a very great poet, very great. He inspired Dante and great works of art. Everyone loved St. Francis. Pigeons loved St. Francis. Even lay people want to be Franciscans, so you have the Third Order of Lay Franciscans and these people are mostly married. I guess I could have done that.

The way it works is: postulant, novice, priest, bishop, pope. The pope is called *The Servant of God*. But you're always a friar. So, I was a Franciscan friar. I studied the writings of St. Francis, and he believed that theology was a waste of time. Anyway so I started out in the novitiate with a year of training. I had to stay on a 30-acre farm the whole time, a farm with a vineyard. We got two pair of *baggies*, baggy pants cut off below the knee like bloomers, two pair of sandals and two pair of socks. You were called a *Brother* then. You studied St. Francis, the Gospels, rules of order. You had personality training, vocational testing. It was a comfortable way of life, simple not severe. We even made our own adobe bricks. We wanted it to look just the way it did in 1889 on the farm. Adobe is great. It'll last forever!

After one year you made your vows. Altogether I was in for twelve years, including five years of training. I liked the Franciscans. They even sent me to college but I was actually more interested in homes: the buildings, the families, you know. But I did like to read, too.

After five years of training I was sent to the L.A. County Jails System. For the next five years I was a chaplain in the jails. I lived in state personnel housing where the families of some of the guards lived and I didn't have a day off in three years, not one. I was there every day, at first setting up prison literacy programs. I liked reading and one thing led to another.

The first step is the hardest, getting into a cell block. It isn't easy to get into a cell block; a person on the outside will have a hard time getting past the Visitors' Center. I had to ask permission. I had to agree that if they used me for a hostage the cell block would stay closed. OK, I said, don't. The sound of the doors shutting behind you. That loud clang, it's the worst sound. Believe me, that loud CLANG. You don't want to hear it.

I was in lock-up 12, 14 hours a day. And I found lots of useful things to do inside. A lot of people get lost in the system and a lot of mistakes are made-- just simple mistakes, errors of all kinds, and people get lost. But this thing about homosexual rape in the prisons is bad, it's just bad. In jail you see the worst.

Here's the thing about jails. 90% of the people in jail now wouldn't be there if we had a just society. 10% are just plain perverts, I'd call 'em. You see the worst, you see the whole thing when you've been in the jails and I was in them night and day for a long time, but what I tried to do frequently was try to get guys out of butt-fuck situations. They call it 'shot-gunned,' and pardon my French but let's tell it like it is. So, sometimes I could appear as a character witness for guys and get them out of these rape situations by getting them transfers.

At first, I thought the Franciscans were sincerely interested in literacy development. And I was setting up literacy programs, teaching people to read. Literacy is a big deal. If you can't read... Some people thought my role in the jails was to reduce tension. But that wasn't it. I was trying to be useful, yes, but I soon figured out that sometimes the best thing I could do was listen to people and try to get guys out of these horrible butt-fuck situations. My main role was to stop guys from being raped.

When I was in the cell blocks for long periods of time, I used to let winos sleep in my car. I had the only 'friar car' that wasn't ripped off. But you hear comments like 'I'll piss on you,' and 'I'll pay someone to hit you.' But I think if anybody ripped off my car, whoever did it would have gotten 'hit' by a paid 'employee,' and you can bet on it that anybody who ripped off my car would have gotten *pissed on*.

Maybe I got to be too independent. But I felt like it didn't matter if I was a friar or a priest or whatever. All that mattered was if I could get some guys out of being butt-fucked. I'm out of the Franciscans now. I'm called a *prison literary consultant*. I teach classes and do a lot of *literacy tutoring*, but in reality, what I still do is try to get guys out of being butt-fucked.

I'm married now. But I didn't drop out of the priesthood because of sex. People always ask me about this. I dropped out. It had nothing to do with sex per se-- not homosexual, not heterosexual. Everyone wants to know about that. And I'm sure that there must have been some homosexual guys at the novitiate. You hear rumors, stories about sexual abuse. Probably that happened, too. That could be, but I never heard about it, priests taking advantage of kids and all that. Not at all. The priests I knew were serious about their vows. Most of the men were just regular people, trying to follow the rules. Anyway. Sex wasn't the issue for me. In the end, I just never had a religious experience.

But I didn't enter the priesthood because of God anyway. It was never about God. I entered the priesthood because I wanted to be a good person, be useful. And I did that. And then that was enough. I just got sick of everything, because I felt that nobody loved me personally, intimately. Nobody really loved ME, plain old me. Not what I could do for you, or who I was supposed to be. Nobody loved ME.

So. I'm married now. My wife's Catholic. I'd call myself agnostic. Who knows! We got married and had a baby. Amazing! And we're still married. And God bless her but there are days when I wish I were back in the monastery! Hah! But there are never days when I wish I were back in the cell block.
But seriously. Lots of people are good, nice company people. They have no doubt about what they believe. They don't question anything, at all. They go along with it and they are good, nice people. But I feel like if you believe something, get involved, get into it. Don't let other people lead you around by the nose.

Before I left the priesthood, I mulled it over for a few months with some good people, some good problem-solvers. Then I made my own decision to leave. What I say to people now is: do the best you can do. Get on with things and do the best you can. Maybe you're not a hero, but maybe you can make a positive contribution in some way.

But I feel blessed. I've always had good carpentry skills. So far, I've been able to make a decent living. So now I'm a contractor now. I hire people and I try to be fair with them. People go too far with this "I'm the boss" stuff. Everybody's gotta make a living. And I do a lot of work with migrant workers, farm workers. I figure, this is a good position I'm in. I'm sometimes a boss; and I'm a married man with kids. I'm in a good position to tell other men who are bosses, too: for God's sakes give folks a break. Other people need to live, too. Look at them. Look at you. Think about it. Yep. Now I have a wife and two kids. I love them. I still love adobe, too. It'll last forever!

"I hope this helps you, Edna. But to tell you the truth, I doubt that my story will work in Hollywood. What I dealt with for so long was prison rape. I'll do anything to help you. But from my background in the jails and as an occasional movie goer, people who go to the movies don't want to see men get raped. If they want to see anyone get raped, which is horrible, they want to see a woman get raped if truth be told. The male rape--nobody even wants to think about it never mind look at it on a movie screen, believe me. But check it out for yourself. Go into a prison and talk to people. People will tell you what they think, how they feel. Go to the movies. You'll never see a man get raped."

Nowadays anyone can see any awful thing in a movie or TV show. And it keeps getting worse. Here and elsewhere. In any event, after that interview Edna's mind went blank for a while. November, it was a bleak November.

Chapter 31
"Almost Thanksgiving"

The festive season, the *holiday season,* was about to begin. Time to bake pies and buy a turkey! It was the first holiday that Edna's mother was *Mrs. Blumenthal.* She liked being *Mrs. Blumenthal.* She didn't like being the *second Mrs. Blumenthal,* "but I'll get used to being number two one day," Edna's mother hoped. Edna was trying to get used to thinking of her mother as *Mrs. Blumenthal.* She still hadn't met *Mr. Blumenthal.* Sidney Blumenthal decided it would be best all 'round if he just stayed in Arizona for a while, far away from the first *Mrs. Blumenthal.* The divorce was over, of course, but his first wife's rancor was not.

It was November, almost time for Thanksgiving and Edna's mother was in town! But not for long. The former Eleanor Reilly, now Eleanor Blumenthal, was in El Cerrito but not to celebrate. She was back at home in El Cerrito—to clean out the house and prepare for THE SALE! Some furniture was being moved to Arizona. Some things would be given away to anyone who wanted them. Whatever was left would go to the Goodwill. Then she'd be moving to Arizona, permanently.

"Don't you want ANYTHING?" Edna's mother asked, again.

"No, no thank you, Mom. I don't need a thing."

"OK, you don't NEED a thing. But do you WANT a thing?"

Not *now.* Maybe she would off *in the future* but where would she put it now? There was no place for any more furniture at Mrs. Kleine's and she couldn't afford to rent a storage space, but it wasn't important. The important thing was that the house was being sold. Someone else would move in. Edna and her mother would never live there again. All Edna kept was an old photo album.

"Just give everything to the poor," Edna told her mother.

"You are not still in the convent! You don't have to keep your vow of poverty! But you might want some of these things one day. What about the COUCH?"

"No thanks, Mom. What would I do with a couch? Where would I put it?"

"I give up! I just give up!" Edna's mother said.

Edna and her mother cleaned every last thing out of the family home. Then they took a walk through the empty house, and then Edna had to go to work. Her mother would have given her a ride but her car was packed to the gills and she needed to get on the road. Edna would take the bus to Holy Hill. It was easier for both of them this way. And so, they said good-bye.

"See you in Arizona!" Mrs. Reilly said, as she waved Edna good-bye. "Hasta la vista, baby!" Whew. She lit a cigarette, and drove away.

"Happy Thanksgiving!" they both hollered out. "I love you!"

Her mother went in one direction, toward Arizona. Edna went in the opposite direction, to work. She found a nice private seat in the back of the bus and cried as quietly as possible. Although Edna had chosen to live almost completely isolated from her mother and the house in El Cerrito for almost twelve years but when they were gone, she felt bereft. After a few moments of nose blowing she collected herself and began to think. She began to think of other relatives she had. On her mother's side, there were no more relatives. Her mother had been an only child and her parents had been only children. But on her father's side, there were lots of REILLY'S.

Most of the Reilly clan lived in Pennsylvania or in New Jersey. Among them was Dorcas Reilly, the creator of Green Bean Casserole. She'd grown up in Pennsylvania and moved to New Jersey after college to work at the Campbell's Soup Company, developing recipes for use with Campbell's Soup. Edna had never been to New Jersey. She'd never met her cousins or aunts or uncles there. Well, some of them had attended her father's and her brother's funerals but for Edna those funerals were just a blur. She wanted just to erase it. Her father was dead. Her brother was dead. Now Edna was the only living child of a widow. And instead of getting married and having children, she went into a convent. Now she was 30 years old. Well, pretty soon it would be Thanksgiving. She contemplated her situation and that of the others around her. Mrs. Kleine had no children. Dr. Q didn't, that she knew of, and neither did Brother Flynn or any of the Jesuits that she'd met.

115

Plenty of people had no children. And it was Thanksgiving, something happy to think about! And if you had few relatives, you could always join in with your friends. At least Edna had Mrs. Kleine, and to an extent, Dr. Q.

"Should we invite Dr. Q over for Thanksgiving dinner?" Edna asked Mrs. Kleine.

"No, he hates me!"

"He doesn't hate you!"

"Yes, he does. He hates me. I'm sure of it."

Edna convinced Mrs. Kleine that Dr. Q did not hate her. He was very fond of her. She was one of his dearest and closest friends. If you say so, OK, Mrs. Kleine relented. On impulse, Edna decided to go for it, be bold. She just went ahead and invited Dr. Q and Harold over for Thanksgiving dinner and they accepted! Fun! (kind of)

The next morning, Edna had to face the fact that she'd invited people over for Thanksgiving dinner and she'd never cooked a turkey before in her life. She knew nothing of turkeys. Edna knew how to make muffins, but little else. In the convent other people cooked the dinners. She'd have to look up recipes. She'd have to go to the market and get a turkey and other things, who knew what? And it was sleeting out. The Good Food Market was only a couple of blocks away but there was no sign of the storm letting up. Half rain, half sleet. Could it get any worse? Edna was ashamed of herself but she wished she'd never invited anyone over for dinner, not have to go shopping, and not have to look up recipes in a cookbook.

"Why didn't I go to Arizona?" Edna wondered silently. "It's nice and sunny down there, 75 degrees. If I were in Arizona, I wouldn't have to cook." Edna's mother had always enjoyed cooking Thanksgiving dinner, cooking the turkey, the mashed potatoes, and the Green Bean Casserole with canned French-fried onion rings on top. But now her mother was no longer living in El Cerrito and the home was gone. Feeling nostalgic, Edna began to take a walk down memory lane, and recalled something. Edna began to recall that one of her relatives on the Reilly side, Dorcas Reilly, had actually invented Green Bean Casserole. Her father's cousin Dorcas had invented it! Edna got out her photo album with old pictures of her relatives, most of whom she hadn't met, but nobody had written any names or dates on the back of these photos. She couldn't figure out which one was Dorcas.

Mrs. Kleine was busy studying her *TV Guide*. "*Brief Encounter* was going to be on, screen play by Noel Coward," she said, reading from her *TV Guide*. She had the right idea. It was a good day to stay in and watch TV. Edna steeled herself as she prepared to go out in the sleet to buy a turkey. A turkey would be heavy and it was sleeting out. Carrying a turkey et al in this weather would not be fun. It could be dangerous in this weather but she could always take a cab back. She'd never taken a taxi before and didn't' know how to do it, but she could always ask someone. And then a realization came to her: instead of buying a whole turkey she could buy a turkey *breast* or maybe *chicken breasts*. They were smaller and easier to carry. She wouldn't have to take a taxi back. She could just walk. It would be cheaper and less complicated. The market was only a few blocks away. She put her rain poncho on over her jacket, and prepared to face the sleet.

As soon as she stepped outside, the sleet turned to rain. Things were already improving! She headed out into the cold drizzle feeling happier. Since Dr. Q's apartment was on the way, she stopped in to see if he needed anything at the market. After all, it was still raining and cold, hard for him to get out. *And*, it was the holiday season, time to think of others, spread joy and optimism and give thanks.

"Ah, Edna, please come in! What a nice surprise!"

"Good morning! I was just on my way to the market. Do you need anything?"

"Which market, may I ask," he asked, "and what will you buy?"

"To the Euclid Good Food Market, to buy a turkey breast, and a pie, maybe some green beans, or maybe chicken breasts and squash," Edna replied, trying not to cry. She tried not to cry and so she just sat there, silently just letting tears trickle down, so as not to sadden Dr. Q, hoping he wouldn't notice. She felt self-pity, and she missed her Mom and her father and brother. She missed the sisters in the convent.

"Ah, Thanksgiving," he said sympathetically. "But this cooking is utterly unnecessary when we can simply go out."

"That does sound good," Edna replied. The lump in her throat already shrinking nicely. "But it'll be Thanksgiving. Everything will be closed."

"The Mediterraneum (really spelled that way) Café will not be closed! The owners are Italian, not American. They have no special attachment to this very dubious, I must say, American holiday. We can enjoy Thanksgiving dinner at Café Mediterraneum. What do you think?"

Edna stopped to take a Kleenex out of a pocket, blow her nose, and think. With its overhead fluorescent lights, the Mediterraneum Café would not be a very festive place for a holiday meal. But on the other hand, she wouldn't have to cook!

"But what about Harold? We invited him, too. Would he mind going to the Med?"

"Ach, Harold is a vegetarian. He doesn't care about a turkey dinner! But let's ask him."

Harold didn't SEEM like a vegetarian. He seemed normal. I 1958 very few people were vegetarians, mainly only Albert Einstein. Albert Einstein believed that the planet Earth was being suffocated by carbon dioxide and that the best way to take care of it was vegetarianism. Too much animal gas! In any event, Dr. Q called Harold to see how he felt about going to The Med.

"Yes, Harold said, "going to The Med would be a great idea. Nobody would have to cook and everyone could order what he or she wanted, vegetarian or what have you. And I have a Handicapped Parking Permit! I can drive, and park right in front!"

"OK. So, it is all arranged," Dr. Q said. "And since there is no need to cook and no need to go to the grocery store, why don't we read the newspaper?"

Unfortunately, Edna hadn't brought the paper. But this day was getting better by the minute. With nothing else to do, Edna went back to Mrs. Kleine's house to watch TV and Dr. Q came along. "A Brief Encounter," screen play by Noel Coward was going to be on.

"I find Noel Coward to be an interesting dramatist. I can't see the TV of course, but I like to listen to the actors and Bettina does a good job of telling me what's on the screen."

A good time was had by all.

Chapter 32
"Who Was Dorcas Reilly?"
Notes by Edna Reilly

Edna was thinking deeply about Thanksgiving and the meaning of Thanksgiving. She thought about the Native Americans, and food. She thought about Green Bean Casserole, and she thought about her father's cousin, DORCAS B. REILLY, the inventor of the GREEN BEAN CASSEROLE. And then Edna went to the library and did some research in the Readers' Guide to Periodicals. She wrote up the following report:

Who Was Dorcas B. Reilly?
(notes by Edna Reilly, niece)

Born July 22, 1926, Dorcas B. Reilly graduated from college at Drexel University in Pennsylvania, and went to work at the Campbell's Soup company in New Jersey, testing recipes. In 1955, she worked on creative ways to use Campbell's Soup. She came up with several top hits but her all-time top hit was GREEN BEAN CASSEROLE with French-fried onions on top, for crispness.

Since 1955 it has never ceased to be a Classic American Thanksgiving Favorite. In 1955 the Campbell's Soup company considered putting the recipe on the back of the Campbell's Mushroom Soup can. Perhaps they did.

One day off in the future Edna would actually go to New Jersey and meet her father's cousin, the inventor of the Green Bean Casserole. It would be at the very end of Dorcas's life. Sadly, she wouldn't be able to remember Edna or anyone else. Dorcas B. Reilly died at age 92 of Alzheimer's disease, having lived in New Jersey most of her life.

Chapter 33
"Dusting and Vacuuming"

Mrs. Kleine and Edna agreed to split up the chores and clean up the house for Thanksgiving, even though they were going out to eat. They didn't have anything else to do and it was sleeting outside, again. Mrs. Kleine would dust and Edna would vacuum. Edna started upstairs. After vacuuming the second floor thoroughly, Edna vacuumed her way down the stairs, la dee dah, la dee dah, happily vacuuming as she went. Mrs. Kleine caught the spirit and started dusting, la dee dah.

Edna got almost all the way down the back stairway when she stepped on the squeaky stair, the same stair that had squeaked hundreds of times before and which they'd ignored hundreds of times before. Squeak, squeak. Edna got down on her hands and knees to examine it. On closer inspection, she noticed that it was loose. It *wiggled*. On closer inspection, she saw that it was different from the other stairs. It was connected to the rest of the staircase by tiny brass hinges. You could lift it up, like a lid.

Under this stair, under the staircase, was a storage space--a secret compartment! Mrs. Kleine was busy dusting. Edna peered inside. It was dark. She started to stick her hand into the darkness to see what she could find. Mrs. Kleine happened to glance over.

"Don't do that!" she commanded. "There could be rats!"

"Oh!" Edna retracted her hand, immediately.

"Ach, there's just some old stuff in there," she insisted, "and there could be rats!" She happily returned to her dusting. Swish, swish.

Rats, however, would be all the more reason to clean it out, even hire a professional rodent-removing company. This could be important. And Edna had nothing else to do. Instead of working on a book, maybe even a NEW BOOK, Edna went to get a flash light. She found one right under the kitchen sink. The batteries were still good! Instead of working on her book, Edna returned to the dark space under the stairs, beamed some light into it, and stuck her arm into the rat pit, unharmed.

From within the dark space she fished out a bunch of men's white shirts, now all yellow, a few dish towels, a quilt cover, some bath towels, and a package of vacuum cleaner bags--still good! Mrs. Kleine continued her dusting. Dust, dust. She wasn't interested in her old stuff, but Edna was. Edna retrieved an old wool blanket, a nice collection of men's shoes, barely worn, and a neat stack of old cardboard boxes filled with various things.

"Mind if I look through these boxes?" Edna called out.

"No, I don't mind." Mrs. Kleine was busy dusting.

Edna opened a small cardboard box and found a small collection of Mrs. Kleine's Life Books from the early 1950's! She opened one from 1953.

"Mrs. Kleine!" Edna called out. "It's your Life Book, from 1953! Mind if I read it?"

"Read anything you like," she called back, busy dusting.

Mrs. Kleine wasn't interested in her Life Book from 1953, or even the lovely old hatbox Edna found. It was pink with silver stripes and smelled like perfume. Edna found a beautiful little black velvet hat and matching handbag inside; they looked brand new! Under the hat in the bottom of the hatbox Edna found a newspaper, from *1938*. Half was in German, half was in English. It was the shipboard newspaper from The Europa, the ocean liner Mrs. Kleine had sailed on in 1938:

Linz, Austria. March 12th, 1938
Adolf Hitler in Austria
Adolph Hitler on Saturday followed the German army into Austria and spoke to tens of thousands of deliriously joyful Austrians who packed the main square of Linz...

And under this newspaper in the bottom of the pink and silver hatbox, was Mrs. Kleine's Life Book--from *1938*. It was written in an elegant little script with fancy curlicues. It was written in German, so Edna couldn't read any of it. Mrs. Kleine stopped dusting and came over to take a look. But the handwriting was so ornate and so tiny and the ink was so faded that she couldn't read it either, even with a magnifying glass, even though it was her own handwriting.

It was Mrs. Kleine's diary from 1938 but what could they do with it? Neither of them could read it. So, they just put it back in the hatbox and put the hat box back in the storage space. And then they made an appointment for Mrs. Kleine to get her eyes checked.

Chapter 34
"Handicapped Parking"

Things weren't looking so good on Thanksgiving. It was pouring down rain. At least Harold was driving, and he had a handicapped parking permit. They could park right in front! Mrs. Kleine, tote bag on her arm, escorted Dr. Q inside. Harold and Edna followed behind.

Dripping wet, they made their way into the café and found a table. It was only 4:30 in the afternoon but it was already starting to get dark. Just as Edna feared, the lighting at The Med didn't exactly create a festive mood. Overhead florescent lights usually don't. But other people were starting to come in, too. And somehow the atmosphere *was* cheerful. And it was *open*!

"Lovely, absolutely lovely," Mrs. Kleine said.

They took off their wet coats and hats and put them on a handy rack nearby. And then Mrs. Kleine began reading the Thanksgiving Dinner Special from the big chalk board on the wall, "Thanksgiving Special, Turkey Plate--."

"They have dinner menus here," Harold interrupted, trying to get his wooden leg situated under the table.

"Yes," Dr. Q agreed. "Yes, dinner menus are available but everything is *self-serve*."

Edna went to the counter and returned with some menus and a self-serve order blank.

"Wow," Edna noted, "half of the menu is Italian and half is Ethiopian!"

"When Mussolini invaded Ethiopia," Harold explained, "he used mustard gas to get rid of native Ethiopians and replace them with Italian colonists." He knew about this because he'd been in the army during WWII in Italy.

"Yes," Dr. Q added, "and that's why in some places you can find restaurants with both Italian and Ethiopian dishes on the menu. The food outlived Mussolini!"

It was the world of The Med at *dinnertime*. To place an order you had to go to a special little window in the back. Edna got some order blanks and took the orders. It reminded her of being back at Blueberry Hill Bakery. Mrs. Kleine ordered an American Cheese Omelet with Home Fries. Dr. Q ordered Spaghetti and Meatballs. Harold and Edna both ordered Ethiopian *Injera* Bread and Lentil-Spinach Stew. Edna jotted down their orders and took them to the window. When she got back they were still talking about Mussolini.

"Mussolini invaded Ethiopia, but the food outlived Mussolini!" Dr. Q mentioned again.

"I remember Mussolini," Mrs. Kleine said trying to remain cheerful, happy to be in the flow of conversation.

Italy was a sore subject with Harold. He'd been wounded in Italy during WWII, and lost a leg. But before you knew it a loud voice called out, "Edna! Your order is ready!" It was the chef. The food was ready! Edna picked it up at the little window. Soon Everyone was all happily munching away, enjoying his or her meal: American Cheese Omelet, Spaghetti and Meatballs, and Ethiopian Lentil and Spinach Stew. No one had selected Turkey Plate.

When they were finished Mrs. Kleine started to read the "Dessert Specials" from the chak board on the wall when she stopped, suddenly, and looked around. Her BAG! Her canvas tote bag was gone! Had she brought it? Yes, she'd brought it with her, she was sure of it, and now it was gone! Edna rushed to the coat rack to see if it might be there, but it was not. Fortunately, Harold found it, right where she'd left it, on the floor under her chair. But Mrs. Kleine was still worried. Frantically, she started rummaging through the tote bag, which was all *wet*.

"Is anything missing?" Harold asked.

"Is your wallet missing?" Dr. Q asked.

No, everything was there. Her wallet was there. Her wallet was damp, like everything else. She wiped it off with a napkin. But something else was missing; she just couldn't remember what it was. "What about your check book?" Harold asked. "Is your check book there?" No, she never carried her check book in her bag. But finally, in the bottom of her tote bag she found it. "Yes, here it is!" she smiled, and handed it to Harold. "All is well."

All was not well. It was her *Life Book, from 1938.* Mrs. Kleine had brought it along! Oh no! She'd brought it along; and it had rained, hard! Mrs. Kleine's damp tote bag had been sitting there on the floor all this time with her Life Book inside, getting all soggy. Harold opened it and examined it closely.

"Oh, my God!" Harold said. "This journal is from 1938!"

Yes, it was. It had been difficult to read before; now it was *impossible.* The ink blurred. Harold was shocked and Edna felt terrible. If she hadn't found it, Mrs. Kleine wouldn't have brought it along in the rain and it wouldn't be ruined!

"You know, Bettina, it wasn't your fault," Dr. Q said, taking a calm breath.

"Yes, it was my fault--all my fault. My father was a good father. It was all, all my fault."

"You must put it behind you," he said, firmly.

No one else said anything. "Well, let's not let this incident ruin our dinner!" Dr. Q said, breaking the silence. "Yes," he agreed with himself. "So. What about some pudding?"

After enjoying some chocolate pudding, they went home. A good time was had by all, kind of.

Chapter 35
"1938"

Edna looked everywhere, hoping to find more of Mrs. Kleine's Life Books from the 1930's and 1940's, and maybe compensate for having been inadvertently responsible for her 1938 Life Book being ruined. She found nothing. Then Edna sat down with Mrs. Kleine and tried talking with her about 1938, to see if that might bring some important memories back, some of the information that was lost.

"I could take notes and write down anything you might remember, anything you'd like to talk about at all," Edna offered.

"Remembrance, I don't know. 1938, it's all gone now. It's like a picture with many, many holes. I don't know. When I lived in Dresden the whole city was like a palace, with cathedrals and flower gardens everywhere. Later it was all... different."

And then Mrs. Kleine wanted to watch TV. So did Edna. Mrs. Kleine's Life Book from 1938 was ruined, a thing of the past; and maybe that's where it belonged.

The next day, Edna was still thinking about what might have happened in 1938. She began to wonder what happened to Mrs. Kleine's mother and grandmother. She decided to call Dr. Q and ask him if she could come over and talk to him.

"Of course, of course."

An hour later in Dr. Q's living room, they got settled. Edna got out her note pad and a pen. She had a feeling that this might not be a good idea. But she wanted to try. She wanted to give it a go.

"Are you sure you won't mind if I take notes?"

"Why should I mind. Of course not. And what is on your mind this morning, Edna?"

"Well, Dr. Q, it occurred to me, the thought came to me, I was wondering—"

"My dear friend, what in the world have you been thinking and wondering? Let's discuss it! Now. What is on your mind this morning?"

"Well, I was just wondering, um. I was wondering..."

"Ah. You are no doubt still thinking about 1938 and what may have happened to Bettina's mother and grandmother. I can tell you very little, only that nobody knows--no one alive, no one we know of."

"Oh."

"We used to write letters, many of us were writing letters, trying to find people. That's how I met Bettina. She helped me read and write letters. She volunteered at Reading to the Blind after the war. You might try writing to Yad Vashem, the Holocaust Authority in Israel. They might know more."

"Oh." She couldn't think of anything else to say for a few minutes. She wanted to ask him something else but maybe it was the wrong thing; she wasn't sure.

"Edna, is there anything else on your mind today?"

"Well," Edna said tentatively. "I was wondering about your life. I was wondering if there might be anything you might want me to write down--about your life, or your family, something you still think about but never wrote down?"

"No. My goal always was to advance the cause of the Jewish working class. I was never a Zionist. I was a Bundist. My goal always has been the liberation of workers everywhere. I was a socialist first and foremost. I still am. And that is all."

What about his family? She wanted to ask. She had the feeling that this could be a bad idea but she went ahead and did it. She asked. "But what about your personal life? Is there something maybe that you might possibly want me to write down for you about your family. Your parents? Did you have a wife, any children? Particular friends? Something like that?"

"Stories, we have enough *stories*. I tell stories of THE MANY, not THE FEW. Do we need another one? I was a Bundist, first and always. We were Jewish and we were workers. We fought for the rights of workers everywhere. We fought for a better world."

And that was that.

Chapter 36
"Father Hunky"

Edna came to a dead halt in her life: with Dr. Q's history and Mrs. Kleine's history, and with her Hollywood screen writing plans. She came to a brick wall. Just as she was about to devote herself to cleaning the vegetable drawer in the refrigerator when the phone rang. It was Brother Flynn. He had a new ex-priest for Edna to interview! Brother Flynn had already spoken to him. His real name was Jean-Claude but everyone called him "Father Hunky". As it turned out, Father Hunky made Edna nervous. He was drop dead gorgeous. But she did her level best to ask questions, listen and take notes. The resulting interview was rather extensive but went something like this:

"Interview #4 with Former Father Hunky"
(as told to Edna Reilly)

"In elementary school I was always a cute kid, with dimples and long eye lashes. My mother was French so they named me *Jean-Claude* just to make things difficult, but everyone called me "Chuckie." In high school I got more macho. I was on the football team. By senior year I was the captain of the football team. They called me "Chuck."

Nobody called me to play pro football, but plenty of movie agents did. This is California, and Hollywood isn't that far away from Burbank. I grew up in Burbank. I don't even know how these agents found me. It wasn't that I was a great football player; I just looked like one. I was photogenic. Girls followed me all over. AGENTS followed me all over. I could never be alone.
Now let me say this. I am a Christian. I'm also a Jungian. I like the ideas of Carl Jung. What I've learned is that we're under a system of symbols in this culture; you can't escape from it. The trouble is that people are very easily managed under this system of symbols and tend to behave automatically, instinctively, without thinking. We are largely controlled by a system of symbols. We can't help it.

I couldn't help it. I just happened to grow into our culture's image of a perfect MAN. I just happened to look a certain way. I had the right image. I grew up thinking I was God's gift to the world. Anyway, so giving my life to God seemed like the natural thing to do, the right thing to do--at least the better thing to do. You could do *worse*. What else was I going to do, go to Hollywood and be a male sex symbol?

Anyway, I wanted to be a priest for its own sake, but it was also a convenient escape from GIRLS. They followed me around! I can't tell you how annoying this was. I could never be alone. And no, I wasn't homosexual. I'm sure men watched me, too, but I just wasn't *that way*. Homosexuality is still a big secret at this time, a big taboo. The whole thing about attractions and sexuality, it's a big deal, but we are only scratching the surface now. I guess if I were THAT WAY my life would have been even more complicated. Anyway.

A friend of mine and I entered the priesthood together. We both had it all. We came from money and we were good looking, and we wanted to be good people. So, we joined the Paulists and became parish priests. It's exactly what I wanted to do. But let me tell you, the parish guys are at the bottom of the pile status-wise in the priesthood. Seriously. Really. It was a challenge to my ego, yes. But in another way, it was just what I needed. That's not to say that I LIKED it.

I ended up going over to the Jesuits. I met some professors who influenced me. They said, "Why not finish your education?" I thought I had finished my education but I hadn't, not by a long shot. I continued my studies and my spiritual training with the Jesuits. I took all kinds of classes. The more I read and studied and prayed and meditated the more I couldn't get around this thing about the infallibility of the Pope.

All Catholic priests have four vows: poverty, chastity, and obedience in general. The fourth vow is absolute obedience to the Pope. But here in 1958 in matters of faith and morals the Pope is taking us forward into the 16th century! Maybe things will change one day, but you don't live forever. How long could I wait for the Church to change? Know what I mean?

It gets back to the Manichean idea of good and evil. The usual thinking of the Church is: the spirit is good and the body is bad. Heaven is good and the earth is bad. That's where lots of people are with religion. They call this "Original Sin" but one day people will figure it out.

So, then you add celibacy into the mix. In the priesthood celibacy is set up for the sake of the institution, the Church. It was originally supposed to be for the benefit of the individual practicing celibacy, no hooks of a relationship to interfere with your devotion to God. That was part of the draw for me, the draw of the priesthood. The priesthood was a haven.

In any event, I was a parish priest but in time I wanted to go beyond the boundaries of a community leader, which is what a parish priest is. I began to feel that I could best serve God by teaching and I was attracted to the Jesuits. The Jesuits encouraged me to keep studying. I took classes and eventually went over to the Jesuits. I continued my education and fully expected to be teaching at some point. I took lots of classes. And then I took a class in Jungian psychology. I started studying dreams and the subconscious mind, with non-Catholics. It was fascinated, doors opened!

I began to see that the body, mind, and spirit were all equally important--and that *women* were important! And that's when I met this nun--in a Dream Study Group and I began to wonder. Why not fall in love with this woman? Why not *love*? It was only healthy! And so, I did it. I fell in love with a nun! And I was still a priest! I was used to people falling in love with me, but I'd never really fallen in love with anyone else before. And I truly loved her and still do. And I'm sure God doesn't mind!

So, we both dropped out and became Jungian psychotherapists. That's what we do. We got married, are still married, and still live together. We have separate practices in the same building; but we share the same belief that men and women are equal and that every person has aspects of masculine and feminine inside. Jung called it anima and animus.

In the end I became disillusioned with the Jesuits. Or, maybe that's unfair. I began to see that certain people got their jollies from pleasing authority figures. I began to see that certain authorities set the curriculum for a tenured core of professors to follow. They call the shots. Of course, some people were more open but I didn't want to give any more of my life to something that wasn't upholding anyone's *freedom*. So, I left the priesthood and I left the church. I refused to be part of the boy's club any more.

Later I understood that there is a certain element of the adolescent, of undeveloped stuff in most priests. And I came to see that the marriages of some priests who dropped out and got married got really hellish! Our egos are undeveloped and our ability to compromise and appreciate women was not there. Dream groups, believe it or not, are a good place to start. They can show you what's behind your thinking. We call it the 'Shadow Side' but of course nobody in the Catholic church will be too interested. And that's about all I've got, Edna."

Chapter 37
"Saying Grace"

One of St. Ignatius of Loyola's most popular suggestions was to "find God in all things." But HOW? In his "Spiritual Exercises" St. Ignatius' included some *Rules* on how to do this, how exactly to find God in all things, get closer to God, and be a better person. St. Ignatius' spiritual tools were designed to help you look into your heart and soul--and DISCERN right from wrong, good versus evil, Christ versus Satan.

One day while Edna was discerning good from bad, she heard a voice, a high-pitched kind of soprano or alto. She thought it could be the Voice of God but that was unlikely. The voice sounded a lot like Edna's own voice, but not quite.

"Hello, Edna?" the Voice repeated. "It's me, the Voice of God speaking."

"God, is it you?"

"Yes, my child. It is I. Don't I sound familiar?"

"Too familiar. You sound like ME!"

"Yes," the Voice of God agreed, "I am using your voice."

"Why my voice?"

"Because I'm trying to help you find your TRUE SELF. It's time for you to DISCERN, to make some critical decisions. Are you ready to move forward?"

Edna paused for a minute to consider, and decided that she was probably NOT ready to move forward. And, after all, she might be suffering from illusions. But then she changed her mind. "Yes, God, I'm ready, really ready!" she called out, too late. The Voice of God had already disappeared, vanished into thin air.

"Wait, wait!" Edna entreated, but it was too late.

God had been offended, insulted. God had vanished, into thin air. And then that old familiar tired listless feeling returned to Edna. She wanted to go back to bed. But she had things to do. She had to clean the refrigerator. It was time for Edna to face something, but from her point of view all she was facing was Mrs. Kleine's refrigerator. Should she clean the whole refrigerator, or just the vegetable drawer? There were choices, decisions to be made every day. Edna decided only to clean the vegetable drawer. As she was preparing to go to work, the phone rang. It was Brother Flynn ("Harold"). He wanted to know if she and Mrs. Kleine would like to join him for lunch at the JSTB cafeteria.

"I know this is last minute, but it's nice and quiet here now, Christmas break time. Want to join us today? Former Father Tom might join us, too, if he can get away from the Reception Desk. Are you in?"

"Yes, and I'll ask Mrs. Kleine, too"

"The more the merrier!"

Edna was delighted to escape from cleaning the vegetable drawer. A few hours later she and Mrs. Kleine were walking up the stairs past the cement lions and into the Administration Building. As soon as Edna stepped inside, she began to feel very tired again, and listless. She wanted to go into the Lounge and lie down on a bench. But she trudged onward. Nobody was at the front desk so they just kept walking through the Administration Building and around back to the cafeteria.

"I am not Catholic," Mrs. Kleine objected, when she realized where they were. "I am Jewish. There has been some mistake."

"No," Edna countered. "*Harold* invited both of us to lunch. And besides, all Christians are Jews, too."

"But I'm a Jew, a REAL one. I will wait outside."

"No, no. *Harold* will be waiting for us. We are his guests."

"Well, in that case."

There were only a few people in the cafeteria that day. It was Christmas break time. A large Christmas tree sat in a corner, undecorated. There was no sign of Brother Flynn, just a dozen or so priests all wearing their *blacks*. They looked up briefly and returned to their lunches. Most of the tables and chairs had been cleared away so the wooden floor could be refinished.

Edna wished she never come here. She wished she'd never set foot in the Jesuit School of Theology. She wasn't part of it and they didn't like her. Fortunately, she didn't know how much they didn't like her. And now here she was, back in the cafeteria, again. But it was Christmas time. Not as many people were here. And it would be nice to have lunch with Brother Flynn. When Edna worked there, she could never eat lunch with Brother Flynn. They had to take turns to cover the front desk. Edna soldiered on. Mrs. Kleine felt unhappy, too. She was nervous.

"I will wait in the other room."

"There is no other room. Come on. Harold invited us as his special guests."

"Well, I *suppose.*"

Edna forced herself to guide Mrs. Kleine thru the serving line, collecting trays and utensils. Because it was a Friday there were two choices: Fish Sticks, or Tuna Mushroom Hot Dish with Green Bean Casserole. They went for the Tuna.

"Ah, Tuna Casserole AND Green Bean Casserole! That sounds absolutely delicious," Mrs. Kleine beamed, scooting her tray along.

"Yes, delicious," Edna agreed, vapidly. Vacantly she picked up hers and Mrs. Kleine's entrees, their beverages--little cartons of Tropical Paradise Fruit Punch--and *cinnamon buns* for desert. Every step required a massive effort on Edna's part but she kept on going. Just when she was about to give up and go home to lie down, a friendly voice rang out!

"Edna, we're over here!"

It was Former Father Tom, saving a table for them! Former Father Tom had a loud voice, hard to miss. He greeted them and helped them get situated. Former Father Tom was the person who took Edna's job after she left. He had been the subject of her first interview. She was happy to see him, and he was happy to see her. And since it was Christmas time nobody had to sit at the reception desk.

"Edna and Mrs. Kleine! It is so good to see both of you!"

"And so good to see you, too," Mrs. Kleine beamed. "My name is Bettina."

"That IS a beautiful name. My name is Tom, and Brother Flynn will be here in a few minutes," he said.

"That's nice," Mrs. Kleine said. "And who is Brother Flynn?" Mrs. Kleine asked, turning to Edna.

"*Harold*," Edna explained.

"Ah, *Harold*! I see. But he is not here and our food might get cold. We might as well get started, shall we?"

"Why not?" Former Father Tom agreed. He was hungry, too. They could always chit-chat later.

Mrs. Kleine picked up her fork--just as Harold rushed in, waving and calling out to them. "I'm here! I'm here!" He hurried through the serving line, collected his Tuna Casserole and his Green Bean Casserole, his Tropical Paradise Juice and cinnamon bun and joined his friends.

"So sorry to be late," he apologized.

You are not late at all, Harold," Mrs. Kleine beamed. "You are right on time!"

"Yes," Edna agreed, staring into space. She didn't care what time it was. She didn't care what they had to eat. She had no appetite. Edna wanted to lie down. But she soldiered on, and prepared to eat lunch.

After a moment of introductory chit-chat, Mrs. Kleine picked up her fork again, still hoping to take a bite before her food got cold. But Former Father Tom and Brother Flynn had already folded their hands and got ready for someone to say grace. Edna looked up and surveyed the room. She had a funny look on her face. Something inside Edna just seem to snap. She started to look happy for some reason, actually happy. For a minute she tried to keep it to herself but everyone noticed. Something was wrong with Edna but they kept it to themselves. Nobody wanted to embarrass her socially by stating the obvious. But something was wrong with Edna.

"Would someone like to say Grace?" Brother (*Harold*) Flynn asked, with false cheer.

"As a matter of fact, I would like to say Grace," Edna replied. She collected all their little cartons of Tropical Paradise Juice and cinnamon buns and put them in front of her. "Let us bow our heads," Edna began, in a noble soprano voice.

For some reason everyone at the table did as she commanded. There was definitely something wrong with Edna. Why was she smiling so much? They bowed their heads, and expected Edna to say something like "Bless us, oh Lord, for these thy gifts which we are about to receive..." But instead Edna said:

"Communion is one piece of bread we share to remind us of what we are, all part of the body of Christ. Christ is present at transubstantiation, not just in memory, but in actual presence. Christ is present in us, all of us, as we live within one another."

"What are you doing, Edna?" Brother Flynn interrupted.

"I'm saying Grace, a ritual of thanks and appreciation to honor our food and our common humanity."

"Can you do it more quietly? People here will think you're crazy, like you're trying to say mass! This will be regarded as a sacrilege."

"He's right," Tom said. "Transubstantiation is a cornerstone of Catholic ritual. You shouldn't be joking about it."

"I'm not joking," Edna replied. She had simply and suddenly discerned something important. She picked a few raisins off her cinnamon bun, held them up in the air, and began again:

"Here is a piece of fruit so I can be fruitful to other people. This is the sacredness of the ordinary. The sacredness of a cinnamon roll and a raisin, the inherent sacrificial nature of the universe so that life can go on. Communion is one piece of bread that we all share to remind us of what we are, all part of the body of Christ. Christ is present at transubstantiation, not just in memory, but in actual presence. Christ is present in us all as we live with one another."

"Edna," Tom interrupted, again, looking around. "There aren't that many people in here today, but the ones who are here are starting to stare. This WILL be regarded as a sacrilege. You are making a mockery of the mass. Are you going insane?"

Maybe Edna was going insane, or maybe just experiencing enlightenment. Depends on your point of view. Something just seemed to come over her, something snapped, a sudden impulse from out of nowhere spoke to her and told her to conduct an informal mass at the table. It made perfect sense to at the moment. Why not? Priests did it every day. And what was to stop Edna from doing it now?

"I may be completely crazy," Edna acknowledged, "but why can't women say mass? And anyway, this isn't exactly *mass*. I'm just

saying *grace*." And with that she gave each person a raisin and a
container of Tropical Paradise Fruit Punch and began again:

I believe in the priesthood of all people, and the common
breaking of bread, and cinnamon rolls, and the drinking of Tropical
Paradise Fruit Punch as we nourish ourselves and one another."

"You already said that," Mrs. Kleine mentioned.

Mrs. Kleine picked up her fork again; she still hoped to take a
bite of food before it got cold but Edna was just getting started, just
starting to feel really happy two large men in brown robes entered the
cafeteria. They made a bee-line straight for Edna and gently but firmly
grasped her by the elbows, lead her away. Mrs. Kleine, Former Father
Tom and Brother Flynn all sat frozen in their seats staring at each other
in shock. Poor Edna had gone insane.

"We'd better go help her," Tom said.

"Yes!" Brother Flynn agreed.

"Yes," Mrs. Kleine agreed. "Maybe we can get our lunches to
go."

Chapter 38
"Holy Hell. Edna, Banned!"

Edna thought that any open-minded person could see the positive spiritual significance of what she had done, especially Jesuits. Hadn't she seen God in all things? The beauty of God in a raisin? And why not celebrate the miraculous nature of transforming material energy into spirit and offering it to God? God had wanted Edna to do what she did in the cafeteria, she was certain. But nobody in the cafeteria could understand it. And after sleeping on it and taking more time to *discern* more deeply, Edna couldn't understand it either.

Why did she do it? Did the devil make her do it? Was she having a nervous breakdown? Edna felt sorry for herself, a wee bit. Who enjoys being rejected? But she still had inner strength, and her steadfast belief in God. Thy will be done! It was not the end of the world, not yet. It was just the end of *something*. She sat quietly and listened to the cold rain outside Mrs. Kleine's warm house as it splattered on the windows. She was NOT in *Holy Hell*, still just on *Holy Hill*, at least on the edge of Holy Hill, enjoying the warmth of Mrs. Kleine's cozy house and her bed. At least she had a bed. At least she wasn't burnt alive at the stake as a heretic or had her breasts torn off by The Inquisition. She just seemed to be running out of options.

In 1958 there were few options for a woman like Edna, a homely woman with poor social skills and a lousy typist, and so she took to her bed. Just like Mrs. Kleine's mother did. For many women, going back to bed seemed like a good option, in a world that didn't particularly want them.

"You have your whole life ahead of you," Mrs. Kleine said to Edna, locating her upstairs in her bed. "At least you have some of your life ahead of you. At least some of it."

"I know," Edna mumbled, barely able to speak. "I feel so all alone."

"You have me! I will be your friend for life. My life will not be as long as yours, but it's better than nothing."

"I know," Edna replied, "and I will be your friend for life, too."

"Just don't be like my mother. Sometimes she stayed in bed all day and wouldn't even come down for meals. She just stayed in bed all day eating chocolates. She became clinically depressed. She let herself go and got heavy. Fat, she got FAT. Do you want to get FAT?"

The next day Edna was still in bed. By mid-afternoon Mrs. Kleine was getting so worried that she went to fetch Dr. Q. That nice young woman, that student living upstairs in her house didn't look well. She looked ill. Should she call a doctor? Could he come over and take a look? At least she could still remember what she wanted to tell him.

"Of course, Bettina. I'm blind but I'll take a look, not that I'll be of any help; but I'll be right with you."

"Marvelous. That is marvelous."

It took a while for Dr. Q and Mrs. Kleine to make the journey across Mrs. Kleine's yard. By the time they arrived Edna was already out of bed and cleaning the vegetable drawer. Sometimes cleaning can be therapeutic, doing some simple activity and thinking about nothing else. This is now called "Mindfulness." As she cleaned, Edna sang an old favorite hymn that few non-Catholics would appreciate:
"Gather round, ye sons of God,
Hear his holy word.
Gather round the table of the lord,
Eat his body, drink his blood,
And we'll sing a song of love!"

Since she was alone, she believed, she belted it out just like she used to do in the choir when she was still in the convent. Dr. Q and Mrs. Kleine could actually hear Edna singing out in the front yard. Dr. Q could not believe his ears.

"Edna, is it you?" he called out once they got inside.

"Yes, it is I!" she called back from the kitchen.

"Is something bothering you, my dear friend? Eat his body, drink his blood?"

"No, nothing. All is well!" Edna washed her hands and emerged from the kitchen. The vegetable drawer was tidy and sanitary, and she was happy to see Dr. Q again. It had been a few days.

"'Eat his body, drink his blood and we'll sing a song of heaven'?!!!"

"It's not *Sing a SONG OF HEAVEN*. It's *Sing a SONG OF LOVE*. That's the way it goes."

"Might I ask. Have you been drinking?"

"No," Edna said, laughing. For some reason that tickled Edna's funny bone. No, she never drank. "No, but maybe I should try it some time."

While Edna and Dr. Q chatted in the kitchen, Mrs. Kleine had the feeling that it was time for The Afternoon Movie Classic. She checked her *TV Guide*, and checked her watch. Yes, she was right! Today's movie classic would be *Blonde Venus* with Marlena Dietrich! It was part of the Marlena Dietrich Film Festival.

"Ah, Marlena Dietrich!" Dr. Q exclaimed, making his way into the living room. "She fought with the Allies, you know, and became an American citizen."

"I believe she was a Lesbian," Mrs. Kleine added.

"She may have been," Dr. Q replied, "or AC-DC as they say. She became a star during the Weimar and went to Hollywood."

"I'm going to Hollywood one day," Edna declared. "I feel it in my bones." She was on an upswing, sometimes called "manic."

"Yes, you will go to Hollywood one day," Mrs. Kleine agreed. "Absolutely. I have no doubt whatsoever."

The movie had already started. But everyone gathered 'round the TV and tried to figure out what was happening. Since he couldn't see, Mrs. Kleine narrated each scene as it happened, giving him the play-by-play of the action.

"Here is a person parading around in a gorilla costume," Mrs. Kleine narrated. "The person is parading around the center of a nightclub floor. Now the person is removing the gorilla suit. And it is a woman, Marlene Dietrich. She is singing "Hot Voo Doo, Hot Voo Doo" in a deep and throaty voice."

"Thank you, Bettina. I can hear it perfectly. She always sings slightly off-key."

"Now Marlene Dietrich is stepping out of her gorilla suit, stripping down to a golden bathing suit and a crazy blond wig. A chorus of ersatz African natives backs her up--in tune."

Then it was time for a commercial break and for Thin Mints but the box was empty! Edna was feeling better. Feeling energized again, she dashed off to the kitchen. She came right back with a new box of Thin Mints. They were right in the oven where Mrs. Kleine left them. Everyone was happy.

Chapter 39
"Who?"

Edna's #4 interview with Former Father Hunky proved to be her last interview. She had not been arrested for trying to say mass at the Jesuit cafeteria; she was just a pariah, unpopular and unwanted. Banned. Her relationship with Brother Flynn chilled, froze. Where could her book go from here? Edna was out of favor; none of Brother Flynn's friends would want to talk to her, not now. All she had was four interviews under her belt. In Edna's opinion all four were excellent. Four interviews, however, did not constitute a BOOK. What good were they? Oh well. Most people would rather watch TV anyway, Edna *discerned*.

Just as she was about to throw all four of her interviews into the trash, she came up with a new idea. She could add some new and refreshing sections. Perhaps a series of short biographies, stories of people of note in history—and then during the late 1950's. Some could be famous or infamous. Some could be unknown, but discovered by Edna. And so, she spent many hours and days in the Berkeley Public Library, reading and taking notes. Every day she started to feel better, more cheerful, more optimistic. A new book started to shape up in Edna's mind. She decided to call it *Who?* The title *Who's Who?* was already taken. Here are a few excerpts now:

"Who Were the Women Jesuits?"
There were two:
#1.) 1542. Isabel Roser was a noblewoman from Barcelona. After her husband died, she went to work with Ignatius Loyola as he was building up his organization the Society of Jesus (SOJ). Ignatius put her in charge of a place called Martha House. She called it a "convent" and kept servants and possessions there. She petitioned Pope Paul III to be admitted to the Society and her wish was granted. Ignatius Loyola didn't think this situation worked out. Perhaps he kicked her out. Perhaps the pope kicked her out, or perhaps she quit and went to a Franciscan convent after that.

#2.) 1552. Juana of Spain, second daughter of Emperor Charles of Spain, married the heir to the throne of Portugal. He died. She was 19 and asked to be a member of the Society of Jesus. At some point she became Regent of Spain to her brother Philip II of Spain. The Emperor would have been angry if she'd become a member of the Society and so she was admitted secretly. She died at age 38, the only woman to have spent a large percentage of her life as a Jesuit.

"Who Was St. Francis?"
1182. St. Francis was born in Assisi, in what is now called Italy. In 1939 during the Fascist era, the Pope made St. Francis the patron saint of Italy. Saint Francis represented love, simplicity and appreciation of all life including plants and animals. One day a Catholic pope might be known as "The Bird Pope." Maybe he would be a Jesuit! Who knows!

"Who Was Galileo Galilei and Who Thwarted Him?"
Galileo Galilei was a leader in the early field of astronomy. He invented the telescope, and discovered the four moons of Jupiter. Jesuits and even Pope Urban VII supported Galileo up to a point in the year 1615 when he was suspected of being a heretic by The Inquisition. The Spanish Inquisition was originally supervised by people from the Dominican order. This was at a time when Jesuits didn't yet exist. Some Jesuits (not all) were later involved in the Inquisition. Some Jesuits (not all) resisted. But that was as far as the Jesuits or Pope Urban VII could go with him. Galileo was eventually arrested. In lieu of being tortured to death he decided to recant his position about the Sun being the center of the Universe. He was just mixed up. Of course, the Earth was the center of the Universe. What a mistake!

"Who Was Edith Stein?"
In 1942 *Sister Teresa Benedicta* of the Cross died at Auschwitz. She was originally Jewish but converted to Catholicism.

"Who Was Joseph McCarthy?"
Joseph McCarthy was a Republican Senator from Wisconsin. In the 1950's McCarthy was head of "HUAC," the House Un-American Activities Committee, which accused many people of being and/or harboring Communists, including President Dwight D. Eisenhower. Eisenhower never publicly denied the charges, but fought quietly behind the scenes. Eventually

McCarthy insulted the wrong people, and faded from popularity. He suffered from alcoholism and died of acute hepatitis at age 48.

"Who Was John Foster Dulles?"
He was Secretary of State (1953-1959) under Eisenhower. His brother Allen Dulles was Director of the CIA (1953-1961). He helped affect a coup d'etat in Iran and in Guatemala. In Iran, Dulles paved the way for the infamous Shah of Iran to replace a democratically elected leader. Too bad. And same thing in Guatemala. He helped get rid of the democratically elected progressive president Jacobo Arbenz, and replace him with the dictator Armas. Too bad.

"Who Is Mrs. Mary Knowles?"
In 1953 Mrs. Mary Knowles was a librarian working in Norwood, Massachusetts. In 1953 a certain Herbert Philbrick testified that she had been a Communist. She took the fifth and was soon fired from her job at the Norwood Pubic Library. Local Quakers who also ran a library hired her. In 1955 she was subpoenaed again. In November of 1956 a Federal jury indicted her for Contempt of Congress. She got twenty days in jail and a $500 fine--a lot of money in those days for a librarian. The Quakers raised her salary.

A couple of Edna's personal favorites were:

"Who Was Agatha Christie?"
Agatha Christie was born in England on September 1, 1890. She was a Virgo, sign of detail. She was a mystery writer and sold by now around 2 billion books. She is much loved for her wonderful characters Hercule Poirot and Miss Marple. She died on January 12, 1976 at age 85 during the season of Capricorn, sign of old age.

"Who Was Edna St. Vincent Millay?"
In 1892 Edna St. Vincent Millay was born in Rockland, Maine. She was named after St. Vincent Hospital in NYC where an uncle received needed care. Her nickname was "Vincent" and she was raised by her mother who encouraged her in the arts. She wanted to be a pianist but her hands were too small and so she became a poet. She graduated from Vassar College in 1917 with a BA. In 1923 she married Eugen Boissenvain, a Dutch businessman who supported her feminism. He gave up his career to manage *Vincent's*. In 1923 she won a Pulitzer Prize for poetry that included the famous line "my candle burns at both ends." In 1938 her husband bought her an island in Maine. On Oct. 9,

1950 she died at her home in Austerlitz, NY, and was buried there on the grounds, under the grounds.

"Who Was Saint Edna?"
Saint Edna of West Ireland died in 516CE. Her date of birth in uncertain. She was also known as Etaoin or Eaene. Word has it that she received her veil from St. Patrick himself. She was canonized as "St. Modwenna" in the 9th century. Few details of her pre-canonization are known. There was also a Saint Enda, actually spelled that way: ENDA. St. Enda of Aaron was a man.

Edna was almost done. She put her biographies together and re-typed everything, using capital letters and very wide margins. Her book was still only 45 pages long but it was action-packed. She had a good feeling. She her completed her work. Her project was finally complete, possibly.

Chapter 40
"Good Shabbos"

In Hebrew Shabbat (or *Shabbos*) means "day of delight." It lasts from sundown on Fridays to sundown on Saturdays. But this Friday night was special. It was Shabbat AND Christmas Eve. Edna had prepared a special Christmas Eve/Shabbat dinner and invited Dr. Q. She was just completing the finishing touches and Mrs. Kleine had gone next door to fetch Dr. Q.

Since she was alone and not bothering anyone, Edna began to sing a few of her favorite Christmas carols: "Silent Night," "Oh, Little Town of Bethlehem," "We Three Kings" and "Oh Tannenbaum." She wanted to get in as many as possible before Mrs. Kleine and Dr. Q (who were both Jewish) arrived. She didn't think they'd want to join in on the singing, and so Edna put the garlic bread in the oven and sang her heart out in solitary splendor. Everything was ready: spinach lasagna, tomato salad, green beans, and Cherry Jell-O for desert. It was a dinner she'd often enjoyed in the convent--a real crowd pleaser. Everything was red and green, Christmas colors! But it still didn't seem like Christmas to Edna. No Christmas Tree, no Tannenbaum! But it was the spirit that counted.

Edna put all the food on the dining room table as her guests entered. Perfect timing! They took off their wet coats and hats and prepared to have a fun time.

"We made it!" Mrs. Kleine exclaimed, Dr. Q at her side.

"My but that smells awfully good! Garlic bread, perhaps?" Dr. Q exclaimed.

"Yes. And there will be plenty for everyone!" Edna replied, taking off her old apron. "Is anyone hungry?"

"Indeed," Dr. Q said, as Mrs. Kleine guided him to the table. "And it is Christmas Eve and Shabbat! Did you know that in Hebrew Shabbat means 'day of delight'?"

"No, Dr. Q, no I didn't," Edna replied. "I don't speak a word of Hebrew but I heard a beautiful song once, 'My Yiddisher Mama' and it was very beautiful indeed."

"Yes, very moving."

"Well, everything smells and looks marvelous," Mrs. Kleine interjected merrily.

"Shall I serve everyone?" Edna asked, without further ado. She was in no mood for GRACE.

"Please," Mrs. Kleine smiled as Edna picked up a serving implement.

"Ah, ah, ah! Wait!" Dr. Q said, however. "If we are really having Shabbat it is the duty of Jewish women to begin the ceremony by lighting candles."

Mrs. Kleine and Edna looked at each other. Edna was not Jewish and didn't know what to do. Mrs. Kleine was Jewish but didn't know what to do; either she'd forgotten or never knew in the first place. Her family was only technically Jewish after all, not religious.

"You can light any number of candles," Dr. Q added, hopefully.

On the verge of being annoyed, Edna got up and found some old utility candles under the kitchen sink. Then she put them on saucers and brought them to the table. Then she found some matches and put them in front of Mrs. Kleine. After a mighty struggle Mrs. Kleine managed to light the candles and all was well. Edna began serving again.

"Wait!" Dr. Q implored. "First we have to say Kiddush! Do we have any wine or grape juice?"

"No, I'm sorry," Edna replied. "There is no wine or grape juice. What about some orange juice, would that do?"

"No that would not do! And what about challah? I can smell that we have garlic bread but we need challah. Did anyone go to the bakery?"

There was no challah, only some wonderful Italian bread, *garlic bread*. Edna was getting a *little closer* to the *edge*. She was ready for dinner and Dr. Q was thwarting her, tipping her over the EDGE.

"Please bow your heads," Edna commanded. Dr. Q and Mrs. Kleine froze.

"What is the meaning of this?" Dr. Q asked.

"Bless us, oh Lord," Edna began with her head bowed, ignoring him, "and these Thy gifts, which we are about to receive from Thy bounty of Christ our Lord who was born on Christmas day in a manger. AMEN. And peace be unto you!"

Dr. Q and Mrs. Kleine frowned, silently confused. And then Edna gave another instruction. She was becoming more assertive about leading prayers.

"After I say PEACE BE WITH YOU, YOU are SUPPOSED to say 'and unto you, Edna.'"

"And unto you, Edna," Mrs. Kleine and Dr. Q said, grudgingly.

Fortunately, the food was delicious and soon a good time was had by all. The dinner conversation went something like this:

"Religion, men and power," Edna said. "It's always that way, I guess."

"Women loved Hitler," Mrs. Kleine agreed. "He was like a God to them. Women wept and threw flowers in his path as if he were a God!"

"Yes," Dr. Q had to agree. "He became his own religion. That was the problem with the German working class. Hitler became a God to them, a God! But not everyone went along with him. There were many good Catholic priests who were among the first to turn against him and among the first to be killed."

After dinner there were Christmas cookies from the Good Food Store and Instant Sanka (no caffeine). Everything was delicious, marvelous. Dr. Q could only agree. And then Edna had an idea.

"Since it's Christmas and Shabbat, I thought each of us might give ourselves a present--a *wish*--maybe something we might like to have done in the past but didn't have the nerve!"

"I don't know," Dr. Q said, "and it is getting rather late."

It was only 5:00 but Edna was talking to the wrong crowd. Mrs. Kleine and Dr. Q had both done pretty much everything they wanted to do in their lives, as far as the outside world would allow. And they were tired now.

"It's only 5:00! We started early. We have plenty of time!" Edna insisted. She wanted and needed to make a wish.

"I have a wish," Mrs. Kleine said, however. "I wish that I had played Faust."

149

"But you DID play in *Faust*," Dr. Q piped up.

"I played IN *Faust* but I didn't PLAY Faust. It was a man's role but I always wanted to play that role. It was the, the—the *fattest* roles, the *meatiest*!"

"But you could do it NOW in the privacy of your own home!" Edna suggested.

Dr. Q groaned slightly. He did not want to hear Mrs. Kleine recite lines from *Faust*. But it was too late to stop the momentum. Edna and Mrs. Kleine rushed off immediately to find a copy of *Faust,* the drama. There were many copies in Mrs. Kleine's house, somewhere, but they seemed to be missing. They found *Faust* novels and *Faust* librettos from operas but no *dramatic play*. Dr. Q waited. He had no choice; he was a trapped audience. But when they returned empty-handed, he was relieved.

"Well, that's that. No script. I suppose it is time to go home."

"No!" Edna objected. "We weren't thinking. She doesn't need a script. She has the whole play memorized."

Yes, Mrs. Kleine had the whole play memorized but only in German not in English, of course, but that didn't matter. Dr. Q relented. He was outnumbered. She cleared her throat, took a breath and began:

"Meine Ruh is hin, Mein Herz ist schwer,

Ich finde sie nimmer, und nimermehr"

"And that is Margaret, singing of her love for Faust," she explained. She was about to continue with more lines when the doorbell rang. "Excuse me, please."

Mrs. Kleine went to the door. Edna followed her, trying to be helpful. Nobody was expecting anyone. It was 5:00pm on Christmas Eve but there was a strange woman at the door, someone Mrs. Kleine couldn't remember having ever seen. She took a moment, trying to place her, but the woman still seemed unfamiliar.

"Bettina, are you ready to go?" the stranger said, slightly offended.

"Well," Mrs. Kleine said. She didn't know what else to say.

Mrs. Kleine couldn't recognize this woman turned out to be one of her old friends from Hadassah Sisterhood, someone who had already gone to some trouble to prepare a Sabbath meal and pick Mrs. Kleine up. Mrs. Kleine stepped a little closer and studied her face. She still couldn't recognize her and was embarrassed; but having been a good actress, she put on an ACT.

"Oh, please excuse me. I'll be right with you. I'll just get my coat and purse. I won't be a minute."

And off she went, with a strange woman, a woman she couldn't recognize, off to an unknown destination for dinner, her second of the evening. Good thing they started early. By the time the second dinner began, she might even have room in her stomach for a few bites.

"Do you think we should have gotten her name and address?" Edna asked Dr. Q.

"No, it was an awkward moment but she'll be fine. It's one of her friends from the temple. All is well, I am quite certain."

Silent night, holy night. All is calm, all is bright.

Chapter 41
"Happy New Year 1959"

If Edna hadn't spent so many years in the convent, she would have known about Swanson's Frozen TV Dinners. Everything was put into light aluminum trays with separate sections for each slice or blob of food. All you had to do was take it out of its cardboard box, put it in a hot oven for a while, and presto--instant dinner!

On New Year's Eve, Edna and Mrs. Kleine took their Swanson's Frozen TV Dinners out of the cardboard boxes and put them in the oven. Well, first Edna had to empty out the oven and light it. But it worked just fine. Edna was feeling a little better, singing a cheerful song that her mother used to sing some years ago entitled "Shrimp Boats."

> Shrimp boats are a-comin' their sails are in sight.
> Shrimp boats are a-comin' there's dancin' tonight.
> You better hurry, hurry, home.
> You better hurry, hurry, home."

And then it was New Year's Day, 1959!

"Has anyone spoken to Dr. Q today?" Edna asked Mrs. Kleine.

"Oh, no. He always goes to his son's house on New Year's Day.

"His son's house?"

"Yes, he lives just over in Emeryville."

"Funny. I didn't know he had a son."

"No, we don't see much of him."

"Huh."

At last it was 1959. Mrs. Kleine and Edna made their New Year's Resolutions. Mrs. Kleine resolved to eat more TV Dinners. Edna resolved to finish her book "Who?" She was just telling Mrs. Kleine about some of her latest ideas when the phone rang. It was Edna's mother called to say Happy New Year. She was still in AA! Her New Year's Resolution was to keep going to meetings and not drink.

"And who needs the empty calories anyway? They're starting to add up!"

"*Easy Does It!*" Mrs. Blumenthal agreed leaning over, putting his mouth near the phone receiver. He'd kicked cigarettes, and was putting on a few pounds himself. "At least we're fat and happy!" he said,

"When are you coming down, Edna?" her Mom asked, upbeat. "We'd love to see you!"

"Yes, when am I going to meet you, finally!" Sidney asked, upbeat.

"I'd love to come down, but I'm trying to finish writing a book!" she said, over the phone.

"A book?"

"Yes, it's called *Who?*"

"*Who?*"

It took guts, but Edna told her mother and Sidney of her plan to write three books and go to Hollywood but had gotten stuck on the first one, entitled "Who?" Edna's mother was delighted. Maybe her daughter would become a successful book writer, and one day be able to purchase her own island in Maine like Edna St. Vincent Millay had--or her *husband had*. It was unlikely that Edna would ever have a husband. She'd have to buy an island in Maine by herself. Edna's mother hoped she would. And then there was Edna's other name-sake, Agatha Christy. Maybe she'd write a series of best-seller mysteries!

"Things at the motel are a little tight," she mentioned (hint, hint), "but we're fine. But what about you? It sounds like something is on your mind. What's wrong, sweetie?"

"I'm fine, Mom. My problem is that my book *Who?*" is a little short. I don't have enough bios."

"That's easy," her mother chirped. "Just write about Dr. Bob and Bill W! You can't miss! And Happy New Year!"

"Thanks, Mom. I'll look into Dr. Bob and Bill W. Happy New Year!"

"Happy New Year," Mrs. Kleine called out from her chair in front of the TV. She was watching The Rose Bowl Parade. So was Sidney Blumenthal.

"Happy New Year!" he called out.

The next day Edna decided that her mother was right. Dr. Bob and Bill W had millions of followers. They helped millions of people. Edna returned to the Berkeley Public Library and researched Dr. Bob and Bill W. She started with some basic short bios, and then started reading "The Big Book," the AA bible, just to get a better sense of things.

Here is the rough synopsis Edna started with. She could always add more later, or change her mind altogether. This was her mother's idea, after all, not hers:

"WHO Were Dr. Bob and Bill W?"
(notes by Edna Reilly)

Leaders in the field of modern sobriety, two American men--Dr. Bob and Bill W--started AA. They were the role models and leadership with the right backgrounds, which Americans could trust: a stock broker and a proctologist. People had confidence in them. Their ideas have spread successfully all over the world. Like St. Ignatius of Loyola, they had a spiritual program that outlined a step-by-step program for overcoming alcoholism and get closer to Higher Power.

Edna researched other significant contributors to the field of sobriety, too. One of note was an Irish priest, Father Theobald Mathew. And here is the short version of his bio now:

"WHO Was Father Theobald Mathew?"
(notes by Edna Reilly

Born in Tipperary, Ireland in 1790, Father Theobald Mathew created an early system to help alcoholics stop drinking, like an early version of AA or the Spiritual Exercises of St. Ignatius. He had around seven million followers in Ireland and in Boston. In Dublin today there exists a Father Mathew Memorial Hall, to commemorate his life and acknowledge his contribution to humanity.

Chapter 42
"The Ascension of Edna Reilly"

Edna was getting ready to go back to the library. Mrs. Kleine was coming along, too. She liked to read the magazines on the shelves. Edna was just putting on her shoes and socks when she heard a different voice. It was a voice like Edna's only it was a man's voice. It was the Voice of God, as Chester from Gunsmoke.

"Hello, Edna. Are you there?" the Voice boomed, kind of but more moderately.

"Yes, God. I haven't heard from you in a while. Where've you been?"

"Heaven. Where else?" the Voice of God as Chester echoed.

"Of course. But you don't sound like yourself, God."

"I'm not myself. I'm Chester, from *Gunsmoke*. He's letting me use his voice for a while. I like it! What then can I do for you, Edna?"

"I was wondering what I could do for you, God."

"Well, before we go there. There's just one thing I gotta say to you, Edna."

"OK, God. I'm listening."

"That's nice. OK then. I know I have a funny sounding voice. I know I have a wooden leg and a serious limp. OK then. But people like me. I am Chester. But ever'body cain't be a Matt Dillon or a Miss Kitty. And even them need some contrasting characters, and that's me. Maybe that's you, too, Miss Edna."

"OK, I can relate to this, Voice of Chester God."

"I know it. Darn it all. But there's just one more itty-bitty thing I gotta ask you."

"OK."

"Could you please JUST STOP?"

"Stop what?"

"Stop working at the library. Nothing wrong with the library but everything in the library has already been done, gosh darn it all! I was hoping that you might a wanted to write something original--about yourself and your experiences in the darned CONVENT."

"Nobody wants to hear about THAT."

"But we do! And by the way, I was hoping for THREE books, not ONE," the Voice of God as Chester kind of slightly boomed out, masterfully.

"Just like the Holy Trinity, one in three," Edna said, trying to lighten things up, "or like the Three Musketeers. All for three, three for one! Or all for one, one for all?"

"This is no laughing matter!" the Voice of God as Chester proclaimed. "I gave you Three Great Tasks and you come up with ONE- -partially completed little inky-dinky thing?"

"For pity sake," Edna begged, "can't you take a look at the ONE BOOK I almost completed? At least I tried my best. Why don't you have a little look-see?"

The Voice of God as Chester agreed to take a little look-see. The wide margins and CAPITAL LETTERS did not didn't fool him. "Pretty skimpy, Edna, wouldn't you say? And I'm sayin' this to you as a friend."

"But it's action packed."

"In ALL honesty I *hoped* you'd write three books but I never really believed it was in you. What I hoped and expected was to get one book out of you, about your life in the convent. Everyone wants to know about the secret society inside a convent, as I've mentioned before now, Edna."

"But that movie *The Nun's Story* was already done."

"So, there's only one inky-dinky nun on God's earth? One and only one little bitty nun's story?"

"I thought priests would be more popular."

"That's because they think highly of themselves. They get out there and make it happen. That's what I hoped you would go on and do."

"I'm sorry."

"Me, too. But so, listen to me. How can I send you to Hollywood to win an award with this flimsy material as your entire resume?"

"Why not? You're God, all powerful."

"Powerful, yes kinda. Stupid, no. There's a lot of competition out there for screen writers. There's a lot of competition for my job, too! Believe me."

"Oh, I believe you, God, absolutely."

"I know you do, Edna. That's why I'm still talking to you. You believeth in me. Look, I'm on your side but you gotta get out of the library. It's full of stuff that's been done."

In the end Edna had tried her best. And more importantly she never lost her faith in God. That counted for *something*. And if God as Chester couldn't grant her an Oscar for Best Anything, God as Chester could grant her a job as staff writer on *Gunsmoke*!

"They still have a few more seasons in them," God as Chester stated. "There's still room for a talented new-comer."

"I love 'Gunsmoke,'" Edna replied. "I love it!"

"I know. And your writing is totally episodic. Episodic is not good for books or full-length feature films but we love a good episode on TV. You jump from topic to topic, and have a ridiculously short attention span. It's just what we need on TV."

And so, Edna Reilly moved to Hollywood. She found an adorable little studio apartment in a 1920's era Art Deco building right on a bus line and joined an affable team of writers on "Gunsmoke." There was one other woman on the team who wrote a few episodes now and then for Miss Kitty basically, but Edna refused to be pigeon-holed. She wanted to write for all of the characters: Doc, Chester, Marshal Dillon, not just Miss Kitty. But Miss Kitty was good.

In 1958 race, gender, and age discrimination was close to 99.9% in Hollywood, though, if not 100%. Three strikes and you were out. Race, gender, age. Edna took stock of her situation. As a white woman over 30 she *discerned* that her chances for success in Hollywood would increase if she posed as a man. Being flat-chested helped. Having no facial didn't. But in Hollywood everything was fake; no one challenged her fake masculinity. Other writers on the team at "Gunsmoke" felt less threatened by a small and short man with no five o'clock shadow and a high voice. Edna decided to call herself "Milton Moore." It had a lilt to it, *Milton Moore*.

She started life as *Edna Reilly*. In the convent she became *Sister Mary Agatha*. Now she was *Milton Moore*. She decided on "Milton" for the poet Milton, and "Moore" for more money. Edna would need more money now, living in Hollywood. She couldn't take the bus forever. One day she'd have to buy a car.

"Hello, Edna, are you there?" the Voice of the Neutral God asked, speaking in Edna's own voice again—that same irritating squeaky voice.

"Yes, I'm here, God. But I don't go by *Edna* anymore; I go by *Milton Moore*. Is this a sin?"

"Call yourself *Milton Moore*. Call yourself *Edna Reilly*. Just don't call yourself late for dinner," the Voice of God joked.

"Thank you, God. I feel better now."

"Great," God continued, "speaking of names, I've come up with an idea for a new series. If it goes the way I think it will, I'll hire you immediately."

"Oh, God, thank you!"

"You're welcome. But when that day comes, you'll have to call yourself *Sister Mary Agatha* again, *Sister Mary Agatha of the Little Sisters of the Perpetual Rosary*. Do you mind?"

"No, Sister Agatha is fine. I don't mind. Call me Sister Agatha. Just don't call me late to dinner!"

After a few years in Hollywood *Milton Moore* got the hang of writing for TV. She made MORE MONEY, moved into a larger apartment, and got two parakeets to keep her company. She called both of them "Poopsie" because she couldn't tell them apart. One day she bought a car.

In Milton Moore, God was well pleased. When God got good 'n ready, God invited Milton to join the team of staff writers for a new show, "THE FLYING NUN." It was still in development. "You might as well join the team now, get in on the basement floor," the Voice of God spoke, using Edna's squeaky soprano voice, "and work your way up before all the others come along and try to bump you out. When you get into a power position everyone comes gunning for you. I'm just trying to be objective here; but going to work is never easy. Am I right?"

"Oh yes, very right. Very true, God."

"Are you ready to change your name back to *Sister Mary Agatha* again? Will that be a problem for you, *Milton*?"

"Yes, that will be a problem, God. I'm tired of hiding behind pseudonyms. Do I make myself clear?"

"Wow, Edna. I asked you a few years ago if you'd mind changing your name back to Sister Mary Agatha again, and you said FINE, no problem. Now you change the deal at the last minute?"

"That was then. I didn't know any better then."

"Well, if you put it THAT way! God was taken aback. "You've changed, my child!"

"I had to. Sitting around the conference table, arguing my plot points, defending my dialogue. I had to write the dialogue, then turn around and argue the points! I had to learn how to speak up when nobody wanted me to. No, sorry, God. No more *Sister Mary Agatha*. No more, no way, no how."

"OK, OK. What about a compromise? Instead of *Sister Mary Agatha* what about *Sister Edna*? That could be even better!"

"I like it," Edna said. "Let's go with it."

In the coming years God could not give *Sister Edna* the *whole enchilada,* but at least she got *a piece of the pie.* It took a long time for "THE FLYING NUN" to take off; but it finally aired in 1967 on network TV. God was well pleased. So was Edna. She finally wrote about her sojourn with the Little Sisters of the Perpetual Rosary convent. Most of it took place in Puerto Rico; but much of the back story took place in Berkeley, up above Holy Hill.

In the coming years these episodes filmed on location in Berkeley somehow disappeared. But in the coming years Mrs. Kleine watched "The Flying Nun" every week on TV with her fellow residents at Leisure World. Sometimes Mrs. Kleine could still remember a woman who used to live with her, when she still had her house on Holy Hill. The woman moved to Hollywood and became a writer on *Gunsmoke* and on this show, too.

159

"Yes, I'm sure of it," Mrs. Kleine told her friends at Leisure World. "She WAS the Flying Nun!"

"Delightful," her friends said. They were delighted to know that their Mrs. Kleine really knew the Flying Nun, and that she could still remember it.

From 1967-1970 "The Flying Nun" was a successful TV series. After the last episode of the last series was broadcast, people watched re-runs for many more years. Some people still watch them now on YouTube. The story was based on the real life of a real nun, Sister Bertrille, taken from the novel by Tere Rios. But God knew very well, however, that several episodes and many scenes were inspired by the life of "Sister Edna."

Well. With her earnings as a staff writer on that show, Edna eventually made enough money to buy a small bungalow in Santa Monica, and it was still on the bus line. But she had a guest room and her mother and Sidney Blumenthal were frequent visitors. In the coming years Edna continued to enjoy her life living and work in Hollywood. Eventually Edna's two bed-room bungalow in Santa Monica was worth a small fortune. When the time was right Edna sold it, and retired to Hawaii. Her mother and Sidney came to visit often. It was very arid in Arizona, and in Hawaii it was nice and humid. Edna always enjoyed their company.

Edna could finally *enjoy* her mother's company, but didn't *need* it. Edna had had so many mothers. She could only count herself lucky. She had her original mother Eleanora Reilly, her Mother Superior at the convent, and her most recent mother Bettina Kleine. Edna couldn't understand it at the time, but Mrs. Kleine had been a perfect final mother for Edna, a wonderful role model who supported and encouraged Edna on her way to Hollywood to become a script writer.

After Edna had lived and worked in Hollywood for a few years she began to see *herself* as a *mother*--a different kind of mother, who had given birth to many episodes of "Gunsmoke" and would continue to give birth to more scenes and episodes of "The Flying Nun." She was a good mother and her children were well behaved. Maybe one day she'd have grandchildren: spin-offs, sequels, prequels. God willing.

The End

JoAnne Brasil is a writer living in Salem, Massachusetts. She has worked as a news reporter for the Brattleboro, VT *Reformer,* wrote an astrology column for *Poets & Writers*, was a letter writer for *Smithsonian*, and hosted *The Practical Philosopher* for WBUR Public Radio in Boston. She was an administrative assistant at the Brookings Institution for one year, and not a very good one. She would like to apologize to everyone on the International Relations floor, especially to Bruce Blair, who worked on the most minute aspects of potential accidental nuclear war. She is currently Executive Editor at Brown Fedora Books.

Made in the USA
Middletown, DE
18 April 2019